# ENTITY

By

DONALD MORRISON

Dark Forest Publishing

ISBN-13: 979-8-9881141-9-2

Printed in the United States of America

Thank you, David "Snapper" Kuntz, for all your input, you gorgeous devil, you!

## Prologue

Pallid, trembling light crawled across the young girl's face, casting deep, unnatural shadows that seemed to hollow her cheeks and eyes. She stared into the camera—no, through it, her gaze pleading, desperate, as if the lens itself might offer salvation. The only illumination came from a battered lamp, its battery nearly spent, its flicker carving the darkness into jagged shapes. In its sickly glow, thin streaks of pink, dried blood or tears, it was impossible to tell, cut through the grime smeared across her skin.

She held her breath, shoulders rigid, hands quivering so violently the camera trembled with her. Words failed her; the silence pressed in, suffocating, as she tried to force out what had happened—what was still happening. Just a month ago, she'd been radiant, buoyed by the thrill of being among the first to set foot on Mars, a pioneer at Attis Station. Now, that light was gone, snuffed out and replaced by a black, gnawing emptiness that seemed to spread from her chest to every corner of the room. Joy had been devoured, hope torn away by the very people she'd once called friends.

Her face slackened, lips parting in a silent gasp as she exhaled, the sound sharp and brittle. Her bloodshot eyes blinked, slow and heavy, before she finally spoke—her voice a rasp, barely more than a whisper.

"Something has gone wrong. The excavation... There... there must have been something inside—something waiting. A virus, or... Oh God... No one knows..."

Her gaze drifted, pupils dilating as if she saw something moving just beyond the camera's reach—faces flickering in her memory, the dead and the missing, the ones she'd laughed with, now twisted by terror and violence. She forced her eyes back to the lens, but they were haunted, hollow.

"People are dying. Everyone."

A sudden, distant thump shattered the silence. The girl jerked, her head snapping toward the open doorway behind her. For a moment, she was frozen, knuckles white on the desk, every muscle tensed like a cornered animal. Her ears strained for the faintest sound—footsteps, breathing, anything that might signal the approach of whatever horror stalked the halls. She knew that even the smallest noise could summon death, could draw the attention of the things that wore familiar faces but moved with murderous intent.

The seconds stretched, the only movement the dust motes swirling in the lamp's beam, proof that the recording hadn't frozen. At last, she turned back to the camera, her voice trembling.

"People are... They're killing each other. Themselves. There's no way to know who it is... what it is. I've never been this scared."

2

DONALD MORRISON

Her eyes locked onto the camera, pupils shrinking to pinpricks, her expression taut with terror. "Listen to me. If you're watching this, stay away. Do not come here. It's in all of us. Everyone. Just... stay away."

Her face collapsed, the last flicker of clarity draining away, replaced by a numb, vacant mask. "I'm so sorry... I wish it could be different. I wish there was another way. But I can't. I just can't..."

She stared at the camera, gaze dropping to some distant, unseen place. After a long, shuddering breath, her hand emerged from her lap, trembling, and set a pistol on the desk. The darkness seemed to thicken, pressing in from all sides, the walls closing around her like a tomb. Claustrophobia clawed at her chest, urging her to flee, but she knew—she'd seen—there was nowhere left to run. The thing in the halls would find her, as it had found all the others.

Her hand closed around the gun, knuckles bloodless, her body hunched and shaking as silent tears carved new tracks through the grime. For ten agonizing seconds, she stared at the cold steel, rocking gently, lost to the horror that had consumed Attis Station. Then, with vacant hesitation, she raised the pistol, put it in her mouth and pulled the trigger.

1

The dark void of space stretched endlessly, a suffocating abyss where even the concept of warmth or life seemed like a distant, impossible memory. The blackness was absolute—colder than death, more silent than the grave, a cosmic tomb pressing in from every direction. In that infinite emptiness, silence reigned so completely it felt predatory, as if the universe itself was holding its breath, waiting for something to stir.

From the depths of this vacuum, a single speck emerged—a lonely, angular shape adrift in the ocean of nothingness. The darkness clung to it, reluctant to let go, as if the void itself resented the intrusion. As the vessel drifted closer, faint markings became visible on its battered hull: TS-163, and the faded insignia of the Earth Military Federation—three crossed flags, their red paint peeling, white stars swallowed by shadow.

The ship slipped past, unseen and unremarked, a grain of sand lost in an infinite desert. Inside, the cold was not merely a temperature but a presence, seeping into every seam and rivet. The corridors were mausoleums, lined with a thin rime of ice that glittered in the faintest light—if corpses could dream, this would be their cathedral. The only sign of life was a feeble constellation of blinking lights at the helm, their glow a desperate, futile attempt to hold back the devouring dark.

*Click.*

A single light sputtered to life in the cockpit, its feeble glow barely piercing the gloom. The sound of electricity crawling through ancient wires shattered the silence, echoing down the frozen corridors like the first heartbeat in a corpse. The instrument panel began to pulse, a faint, arrhythmic beeping that sounded almost like a warning. Deep within the ship's bowels, systems groaned and shuddered as they were forced awake, the hull trembling with a dull, ominous energy.

In the cryo-room, the overhead lights flickered on, their sterile glow revealing a weapon rack bristling with rifles and pistols—silent sentinels waiting for hands that might never return. A thin, serpentine hiss slithered from the vents as the environmental controls sputtered to life, pumping a fragile blend of oxygen and carbon dioxide into the dead air. The ice that had entombed the ship's interior began to weep, droplets crawling down the walls and pooling on the floor, as if the vessel itself was mourning.

Minutes passed. Then, a single red light ignited in the ceiling, bleeding across every surface, painting the room in a sanguine glow. The condensation streaked like blood across the walls and floor, transforming the sterile chamber into a butcher's canvas. The light snapped green, then faded, leaving only the cold, clinical white behind.

# ENTITY

*Pssssst.*

A violent hiss erupted, the sound almost a scream after so much silence. The cryo-pod lids began to open, not with the gentle grace of awakening, but with the slow, mechanical inevitability of coffins unsealing. The white light seemed to recoil from the darkness, monitors flickering to life and displaying vital signs—proof that something, at least for now, still lived. Above, hidden fans sucked the vapor from the pods, as if the ship itself was eager to purge whatever had been sleeping within.

Moments later a hand clasped heavily to the side of one of the pods, and a single body rose.

2

It wasn't Staff Sergeant Baker Thomas's first trip out, nor did he expect it would be even close to his last. He had been an enlisted man from the day he had turned seventeen; the same year Xenocorp had opened their first resort on the moon. He remembered what space flight had been when the trips were too short for cryo, and personally, was happy to be knocked out for the longer journeys. Space terrified him. It was vast, cold and deadly, and what burrowed into him the most, was that even with the colonization of space and long-range travel, humanity still knew nothing more about it than they did when they still relied upon a compass and sexton. He would have preferred to be sitting at the bottom of the ocean than traveling out past the stars. Every time he left Earth he felt it was going to be a one-way-ticket. It was only a matter of time before something happened; fried electronics, a cryo-pod with a faulty seal, a loose weld on the hull. Somehow, deep inside, he knew that space was going to be the death of him. But right now, sitting in the soft interior of the pod, he was simply trying to remember his dreams. As he ran his fingers through his closely shaved hair he struggled hard to catch any glimpse. Scientists were absolute in their belief that people dreamt in cryosleep, their brain scans and EKG readings confirming it, but for every long haul that he had ridden through, he had yet to remember a single one. The only thing that greeted him every time was the same empty feeling that felt as though years had been ripped off his life every time he was pulled back. This trip was no different and he found himself wishing that he had pulled a ticket for one of the newer, faster than light capable ships that didn't require the use of cryogenics for long distance travel.

He took a deep breath and swung his legs over the edge of the pod, letting his feet touch the frigid floor beneath. A piercing chill stabbed in from the pads of his feet; a feeling he found himself unfortunate enough to be familiar with. He sat for a moment, the cold slowly rippling upwards, pushing the sleep back as it did. He readied himself and then stood, testing his legs as he did every time; the continuing fear that he had somehow been out for hundreds of years forcing him to check for atrophy.

*No... just another long haul*, he thought as familiar surroundings flooded into sight.

Behind him the sound of movement signaled another of the group coming awake, followed by a small cough and a sleep-wracked-voice asking if they had arrived. The single question fell oddly comforting against his ears, as another one of his fears was awakening to find that only his pod had survived the trip, and that he was going to drift alone until his sanity faltered and starvation finally won him over. God he hated space...

"Yeah," Baker replied as he made his way to his locker, "another shit trip through space complete."

He didn't share his fears with the others. In that fact, he didn't share much of anything. What his unit knew of him was what they found out through their own digging, or through the grapevine of military politics back on Earth. Fear especially was the one thing he refused to share with them. He had to be fearless, alert and concise in any situation. He had to be their backbone.

"I need a sit rep, Portofino. Tell me we're green."

"You got it, Sarge. First thing," a younger woman with tied back hair replied sharply.

It wasn't regulation for his men to address him with anything other than his rank or name, but his unit had watched an archived holo-movie a few years prior on base, and the characters had referred to their sergeant as such, and after that, his unit started jokingly referring to him as that. It was one of the things that kind of stuck. He didn't mind so much.

He watched the woman with light brown hair make her way to the locker with the name *Portofino* scrawled across the thin strip of tape above. Even though she had just woken, she moved with untapped grace across the floor. His eyes caressed the gentle curves of her body as she approached her locker and moved to click it open. The pilot had been in his unit for the last three years, and in that time they had multiple long hauls together, which meant each time they awoke, or went down, they were stripped to their underwear, and each time, he still couldn't help but steal a glance. The others would joke that she should have chosen modeling instead of the military, that she would have made a hell of a lot more than she did as a grunt. Though he never spoke it, his position and standing not allowing for his crossing of that fine line between compliment and fraternization, every time she made that trek to the clothing hidden neatly away, he stole a glance and couldn't help but agree. So again, he found himself waiting for the moment that she was turned, to graze her form up and down with his eyes before replying.

"Roger that."

Another soldier stepped onto the cold floor and danced between feet for a moment. "God, I hate cryo..." He brought his tongue across his teeth and clicked loudly, scrunching his face as he spoke. "And which one of you assholes shit in my mouth while I was out?"

"I say that every time I go down on your mother," another replied with a grin.

"But Vuong, I thought you only liked men."

"You wish Fascio, you wish."

Another of the unit stepped out of their pod, glancing between the others with a smile, the silence that had held the room captive just moments ago, now a distant memory, melted away with the crystals that had enshrouded them. "How long are we gonna have to deal with you two flirting every time you wake up? You may as well just share a pod at this point…"

Fascio slipped his shirt on, turning to look at the other. "No need to be jealous, Wilkes; there's plenty to go around." He smiled with a wink as he turned to fish out the rest of his clothing.

Jason Fascio had enlisted at the same time as his best friend, Steven Vuong. They had been assigned to the same unit, and when the space corps did the big push to recruit for their program, both had signed up. They had quickly become good friends, and the others in their unit knew that though the pair constantly danced the perimeter of insubordination and harmless humor, when things got tough, as they had in the Rwandan uprising in 2148, there were no two better soldiers to have at their back. Vuong could hack anything with a wire coming out of it; a natural electronics expert, and if you put anything with a trigger in his hand, Fascio could use it to put the eye out of a sparrow at five hundred yards, in the wind. This is why Sergeant Thomas found himself putting up with their interpersonal antics much more than he normally would with other marines. Especially on a trip where everyone's lives depended upon the fine electronics around them being in good working order. Both of them had, on separate occasions, reached a pushing limit of reprimands that left them teetering on the border of discharge, and as badly as he might have wanted to, he wasn't going to find any two better at their jobs than them, so he relied upon more primitive means of keeping them in line, yelling and latrine duty. Right now, however, he was still dazed from cryo, and fighting to keep the contents of his fluid-lined stomach where they belonged. The distraction from being surrounded by space was also a tiny comfort.

"Looks like we're an hour away from orbit, Sarge," Portofino said as she pulled up an image on her holowrist. "Just a little ways out now. And you'll be happy to know, we're green across the board."

"Good," Baker replied, glancing at the small cylindrical piece of equipment that was wrapped at the base of her forearm, before turning to look at his unit. "Chow hall in ten for briefing." He paused. "And a much needed cup of coffee."

"Aye aye, Cap'n," a taller soldier with blond hair that stretched regulation length, replied as he snapped an exaggerated salute.

"Too early, Dom," Baker replied with a growl. "Too early…"

3

"Whatever," Fascio chuckled, as he stabbed at the pile of paste on the plate in front of him with a spoon. "It's all the same shit with different coloring in it."

"Hey," Dom replied with a grin. "If you don't like it, I'll take it. Not my fault you're too good for the slop, princess."

Wilkes started to join in when the last person on board straggled into the cafeteria-style room. Conversations stalled out and all eyes felt to the latecomer. He was of average height with an average build and a face that you would forget as soon as he turned away. The thing that gravitated was the suspicious air that hovered around him, as if every breath he suspected someone or something was going to jump out and attack. The nervous man, dressed in grey slacks and a neatly pressed, collared dress shirt was James Talmadge; a representative of Xenocorp. One of the largest companies in the galaxy, alongside Krieger Synthetics and The United Alliance Federation, Xenocorp was at the forefront of space habitation, and the one that had commissioned the trip they were now on. They had been responsible for building the first tourist attraction on the moon, and the small, encapsulated colony that was slowly building around it. The man standing silently in the doorway was there for the sole interest of the corporation, and the stench of mole was wafting off him like an air of cheap cologne. He hadn't spoken one word since stepping on board to anyone except Sergeant Thomas, and even that conversation had been short. The moment he had stepped on board, everyone in the unit immediately disliked him.

"Mr. Talmadge," Baker said, breaking the silence as he noticed the man taking in all the eyes locked to him. "Grab a seat. We have the finest military feast one could hope for."

The man made his way to the processor on the wall and hit two buttons, one triggering a cup to dispense with instant coffee and another dropping a plate followed by a helping of processed bacon and egg-flavored instameal. When it was finished he turned and made his way to the empty space next to the sergeant.

Baker eyed him as he approached, watching the man's gait, brooding and insecure as he passed the marines that looked at him in turn. He could sense how unnerved the man was, and immediately knew, he had never spent a breath of his life in the company of the military, or probably even a security officer from how nervous he was. Though, something lay silently beneath the mask of uncertainty, something poised to come out at the right moment, something rigid and cold, staunch and accusatory.

The man took a seat next to the sergeant, pulling it in under him and letting his gaze fall to the tray before. The room still held their gaze, fascinated by the awkward man staring down at his plate.

"I trust you slept well," the sergeant continued.

The man grunted, his gaze still held fast to the pile of slop in front of him. "Have we reached the colony?"

Dom leaned over to Fascio who sat next to him and whispered, "Who is this prick?"

"Some fancy suit from Xenocorp."

"Jesus, one of you guys wanna help him retrieve the piece of wood that seems to have lodged itself in his ass?" There was a small chuckle from the table opposite Sarge, Portofino and the rep. Baker could only assume that the cackle was directed at the newcomer and lifted his eyes to the others the briefest of moments, eliciting their silence.

"We're about an hour out, little less," Baker replied, his gaze burning into Dom for a moment, who stiffened up in response.

"Good," the rep replied. "Any contact yet?"

"I've hailed them twice since we resurrected, nothing yet," Portofino answered, pausing with her spoon hung right before her lips. "Still dark."

Talmadge had picked up his utensil, but paused at the pilot's words. He turned his head and glanced at Baker. "Resurrected?"

"Military term. Reserved for space flight. We use it instead of waking up, cause after enough times under for long hauls, you kind of equate the dreamless trips as dying. When we wake up, we're resurrected to fight another day."

The rep shifted nervously, and Baker could see that he was uncomfortable with the reference. He could also see by how he avoided

15

eye contact with the others, as if locking gazes would spread an unseen parasite between them, that talking to the rest of the crew would be a communication relayed through himself to them. There was an aura of arrogance that extruded from him that gave

Baker the feeling the other man was too good to talk to the lowly grunts. Maybe the man just hated the military, some past traumatic event, or another nouveau-hippy war hater. Either way, he despised it when people disrespected his unit, and even more so, when snobby assholes talked down to him from their self-incepted pedestals. Slowly he lifted his spoon and took another bite, chewing for a moment before swallowing the thick paste along with the words that yearned to spit forward.

"So, what's the occasion, Sarge?" Wilkes asked from the next table over.

"Yeah," Corlin said, setting his spoon down. "Any idea why the hell we're being sent out here in the first place? I mean, doesn't exactly take a whole unit to fix a broken radio."

"No," Dom chuckled. "Just Wilkes." He smirked, a grin spreading across his thin face. "Could have just shot him across space in an escape pod and been done with it, saved us all the trip."

Fascio tapped him in the chest with a grin. "Right."

Baker listened to the exchange, his own personal amusement playing into its allowance before cutting it short. "If you ladies are done," he snapped, turning his gaze to the man next to him. "Mr. Talmadge. Would you care to elaborate to the crew why exactly it is that we have just traveled halfway across the galaxy?"

Talmadge squirmed a little bit in his seat at having to address the unit that stared at him with malintent. Inside, Baker took a small amount of pleasure in it. Then the rep set his spoon down and took a deep breath. "So, as you know, the Earth's resources are failing. Oil is already depleted and natural gas is running dangerously low. It's estimated that within the next twenty years, there will be none left. Our company; Xenocorp, has taken it upon themselves to make Mars a livable habitat; a second Earth if you will." A hint of pride slithered into his practiced speech. "We've been building a large community around a central atmospheric processing plant and have been working day and night to create and sustain a breathable atmosphere. We hope to be able to start fully colonizing it within the next twenty years, with additional facilities being constructed upon its completion."

"Save us the sales pitch man," Dom sneered. "We just wanna know why it is we got drug out here."

"You stow that shit, devil," Baker snapped, Dom once again resting his finger on that single button that triggered his anger to rise. This time, the look he gave him closed his lips permanently. The other knew exactly what would await him if he spoke up again, his immediate desire stifled at the thought of his last punishment.

The crew could see Talmadge cringe, and he fidgeted with his hands for a moment before looking to Baker, who took the cue to take over from there. "Wilkes, would you be so kind as to pull up the last transmission that was sent from Attis Station?"

The Lance Corporal moved his tray aside and pushed a small button on the underside of the table. Instantly a hologram image of a keyboard illuminated on the surface in front of him. He typed across it for a second before a holographic image of a vid-screen popped up in the middle of the table. Frozen in frame was an older man in a grey lab coat with the Xenocorp logo embroidered neatly across the lapel. He reached forward and tapped one of the buttons on the keyboard and the video came to life.

"Now what you're going to see here is strictly classified," Talmadge said as the video crackled to life. "No one outside of the company and your commander here has seen this, and it is and will be considered a criminal offense if any of this information manages to find its way outside of this room."

"Yeah," Dom chuckled. "Cause there's a hell of a lot of people around to share this with..."

Fascio and Vuong chuckled, the smile growing across Dom's cheeks. Immediately all three stifled down with a single glance from Baker, who then turned his attention to Wilkes and nodded.

Wilkes pressed the button that began playback and the screen snapped to life.

"Our excavation team found something today. It's huge—unprecedented. We have found irrefutable proof that there was, in fact, life on Mars prior to our arrival; possibly an entire civilization." A smile grew across the scientist's face. "What we have here, is an absolute, archaeological and scientific goldmine. At the moment, we have no idea what it is, but what we can say, is that it is a single, pyramid-like structure, and that it is unquestionably alien in origin. Our teams have done thermal, seismic as well as radio and x-ray scans of the structure, which in design, seems consistent with the pyramids in Earth's Egypt. The results are astonishing. We have found that there are a series of tunnels running through it, with a large, central chamber that they seem to circumvent. There is no apparent entrance, but our excavation team is currently preparing to breach the outer wall at one of the sealed exit points to investigate further. We will send regular updates with any findings we may make, as well as soil, atmosphere and carbon samples for dating. Our initial analysis has determined that this structure has been here for nearly a half a million years. But as our science lab is still growing and some of the equipment we have is not as sophisticated as that which is in the labs back on Earth, we must wait for the shipped samples to be confirmed. We will continue to do as much as we can here, and are all very excited."

Talmadge shifted nervously, pushing his seat out and making his way to the processor on the wall where he filled his cup with water.

Baker watched him take the glass down in a series of gulps, and waited for him to turn around before he continued. "Could you pull up the next one?" he asked, glancing quickly to Wilkes, before letting his gaze fall back to Talmadge who stood silently, staring at the blank screen hanging in the air. He had seen the videos prior to leaving Earth, and the hairs on his arms tingled to life beneath his sleeves at the thought of having to sit through it again. He had sat awake for the two days following before announcing to his unit that they would be shipping out, and clenched on the inside at not being able to share the information to them prior. But protocol dictated that things be kept quiet before they departed; a stack of nondisclosure agreements ensuring his silence. So, he took a deep breath, steeled his gaze and then continued. "The company received this transmission just two weeks before all communications ceased. This next one, is one of the final communications from the colony."

He nodded to Wilkes, who reached out and pressed on another file. A video very similar to the last popped up on the screen. This time, it was a colonist, not a scientist, and the look on the woman's face was vastly different than the bright, smiling man that had spoken prior.

"I'm not sure what they found out there, admin has been pretty hushed about the whole thing. But something's wrong... They found that structure out there a week ago, and now all of a sudden people are beginning to get sick. And that's not all. People are dying. The science team won't say anything, and medical's been quarantined since this morning. I don't know where Kyle is, and Danny... Danny told me he saw his grandmother this morning. She died on Earth two years ago. But the way he described her... We're all scared. The whole facility is falling apart. There's this whisper. Like a familiar voice. Everyone's hearing it but pretending not to. I know it... I'm scared. We all are..."

The woman stared at the screen for a moment when a shadow moved past the hallway behind her, a dark shape in the dim corridor. She tensed, her pupils dilating nearly to the point of all color disappearing, swallowed by the growing black. Then she nodded softly and reached out, turning the camera off.

"What the hell..?" Dom whispered, just loud enough for the others to hear.

A thick unease worked through the room, creeping silence pressing back in between them. Baker didn't have to lift his gaze to know the looks held on his team's faces. He knew all too well the cold knot that was growing in their guts, the tightening of flesh across their backs. Silence screamed between them, the choir of their breath stifled deep within clasped throats behind gaping mouths. An eternity passed, the cold in the air whispering back at them, before the company rep cleared his throat, snapping the unit from their daze and allowing a rush of breath to be expelled into the room. "That was one of the last transmissions we received. Since then, the colony has gone black. So, the company felt as though it would be pertinent to have yourselves and the person in charge of acquisition and appraisal, myself, go see what all the fuss is about. I understand that some of you," his gaze moved to Dom like a snake following the heat signature of a mouse, "are not so keen on this journey, but I can assure you that if Xenocorp finds it important enough to elicit this trip, then it is by far, more important than whatever it was that you happened to be doing before this." He paused, glancing to Baker who sat surprised to see the business side of the snarky man manifest so quickly. But Baker knew it was only in a moment of other's weakness that the man's courage could flare. "Now when we arrive, we will assess any damage or problems that may have occurred with their communications relay, and I will meet with the director to retrieve, personally, any findings that they may have acquired post transmission. The rest of you are here as a just in case scenario."

"Damn," Vuong whispered to Fascio who nodded almost unnoticeably in reply.

The unease that hovered in the air wore thick. Questions were lost in an image of frailty cut short; depleted sanity lost to the echoing crack of a single gunshot.

"Well okay," Baker said, tearing at the thick sheet that had blanketed them. "It's plug and play. We get there, run it by the numbers, and we're back on Earth before we have time to shit out breakfast." He glanced at each of the marines one by one, catching eye contact with each before moving on. "I know none of us wants to be here, but this is what we get paid to do, so let's get it done quickly. I don't want to be out here any longer than I have to."

"I just need to give everyone a quick check up before we land," another woman said, her small voice singing across the room. "Let's give 'em a clean bill of health when we get there."

"I could use a thorough checkup," Dom grinned, a thin layer of insinuation flirting inside his words.

Baker was about to snap when the chief medical officer responded coolly and without missing a beat. "Trust me, DiLeonardo, I've checked that, and it isn't anything worth writing home about."

Baker smiled as the others around Dom's table burst into a fit of laughter.

"OOOHhhhhhhhh…" Fascio said, slapping his friend in the chest before standing up. "And you thought space was cold. Damn… Way to go Lanskey."

Above them a small speaker pulsed to life, a thin rhythmic beeping that hovered on audible, announcing that they were nearing orbit.

"That's our signal," Baker said, sliding his chair out to rise. "You heard the lady. Make your way to med-bay and then find your posts on the double."

4

Baker sat on the edge of a bunk in a small room designated for officers. He had turned the holo-vid over again and again in his mind, trying multiple ways to rationalize it as a singular occurrence, or a case of bad timing; one person cracking from the pressures of deep space mining followed by a communications outing. But there was just something that didn't sit right, something that clawed deeply at him, a sixth sense honed by years in the service that tingled up his spine and screamed from the depths that something was badly wrong. He was about to lead his unit right into a really shitty situation. He could feel it. It was the desperation in the woman's eyes, the loss of hope, and that final moment that must have plunged like a coffin nail into her mind as she made that ultimate decision. Something on that planet had gone horribly wrong, and no matter how he phrased it to himself, no matter how much he listened to the pompous representative's words, he knew it. Nothing good awaited them.

He flicked the edge of the photograph in his hand with his forefinger over and over as his mind compartmentalized their mission, mentally filing things in order of importance and efficiency. He wanted this to be another short trip, out and back with just enough time between for him to force back the emotions the picture in his hand conjured. But the video, the quickly organized trip, the secrecy hovering like a cloud around his assigned mission, and the company's involvement in the whole thing, it all told him this would not be that trip. He could feel it growing in his gut that this was going to be another long one. So, he took a deep breath and exhaled slowly, flicking the picture one last time before placing it in his shirt pocket without a second glance.

*"We're approaching orbit, all hands at stations. Prepare for entry."*

He startled as Portofino's voice crackled over the ship-wide comms. He inhaled sharply, rubbing his face with his hands as he stood to make his way out into the hallway. As he made his way to the bridge, his thoughts continued to revolve around the mission ahead. The rep had told him that they believed it to be a faulty communications relay, but it was his job to assume that was the best-case scenario, and to prepare for what the back of his mind whispered was otherwise. He approached the bridge and took a seat next to Portofino.

Behind, Vuong, Talmadge and Wilkes filtered in.

"Let's see if we can get 'em on the comms," Baker said, his eyes scanning the planet's surface on the vid screen in front of them.

He'd never been to Mars , but as he looked across the reddish orange surface, a nervous anticipation built inside him. He hated space travel, had regretted accepting the position almost as quickly as he had made it, but there was one thing that never got old for him; seeing things that most people only got to see in pictures and holovids. Every time he saw a new planet, or stepped onto new terrain, it reminded him of the second reason he had applied for transfer to the space corp, the first being an escape from the pain he felt when he was back home, surrounded by an empty house, no laughter or faces smiling back at him; emotions torn from him on his last leave, stolen away by an emotionless phone call that his wife and daughter had been killed. A chill ran through him, and he could almost feel the small photograph burning its way through the pocket at his chest, piercing into his heart. He pushed the thought back and pulled his focus to the surface of the planet they were approaching, one that his grandparents had only seen on the net, the same his parents thought would never be set upon. Inwardly, despite the pain that had just been pushed back down moments before and the uneasiness that wrapped its icy grip around him, if only for the briefest of moments, he felt something his years in military service had beaten out of him; special.

"Attis Station, this is military transport vehicle, Tango Sierra One Six Three with the Earth Military Federation. We're here under authorization of Xenocorp to check your communications relay. We are on approach vector and are requesting immediate docking authorization. Again, this is military transport vehicle, Tango Sierra One Six Three, with the Earth Military Federation, please advise."

The crew on the bridge sat in silence, waiting for a reply.

*Shhhick. ZZrrckkreaaaahhhhh!!!*

Baker could feel the pulsing in his chest increasing as his heart began to pump faster. The sound that had torn through the speakers had at first sounded like a garbled static, but there was something behind it, something that screamed of exquisite pain, scraping metal blended with tearing flesh and ecstatic moans. No one spoke as the sound continued. The electric response filled the bridge, squirming between the group. Then the speakers fell silent and the comms became still again.

"What in the hell was that?" Baker asked, looking to Portofino, who stared at the speakers in front of them. His mind told him that it was simply static, but that other part tugged rapidly at the back of his thoughts, insisting that he had heard something else behind it.

"Static, Sarge," Portofino replied, pulling her gaze back to the projection screen in front of them. "Seems like even their short range comms are malfunctioning." Though her words were delivered as a matter-of-fact statement, he could sense the light tinge of a question behind them.

"Did that sound strange to you?" Baker asked, the gooseflesh under his sleeves still tingling.

"Could be interference," Portofino replied, quickly skirting the question. "Probably just a malfunction." She had heard something as well, but she didn't believe in ghosts or goblins, or things that crept in the darkness or hid under beds. She was a science officer and a pilot, the latter taking the forefront only in the three years prior. There was no room for the supernatural for her. If it couldn't be explained, it wasn't real, and the sound she had heard; the images it had conjured... There was no way they could have been real. No. It had simply been static, scrambled by some type of interference. "Gonna be a bumpy entrance," she said, pressing a series of buttons on the curved console before her. She reached out and clicked the open communication button. "All right everyone, we'll be entering atmosphere in minus three minutes. We're gonna hit turbulence so make sure you're strapped in."

Baker reached over and pulled his harness down, securing it with the clasp at his chest. The knot wrapping his intestines tightened. This was another part he hated about space travel. Flying. Even back on Earth he had hated traveling by air. He'd rent a self-driving car before he would ever purchase an airplane ticket. Even though there hadn't been an airline accident in over a hundred years, with all flight and controls having become completely automated, the thought of the possibility still dug deep into him. Even though his wife would tell him time and time again that flying was safer than crossing the street, he still felt the same fear every time. He could feel the sweat beginning to push through his palms and caught his feet turning in towards each other. He readied himself for the part he hated the most.

5

As the ship broke through the outer atmosphere, a low rumble filled the interior of the vessel. In the personnel hold a smile grew across Dom's face as he stared across to Vuong who held his restraints beneath knuckles blazing white. He loved the turbulence; the more chaotic the better, and he felt an electric charge run through his chest at the fear the others were feeling. He wasn't an asshole by nature, or a sadist that took pleasure in others' discomfort, but there was something about the look on their faces that made him for that moment feel just a little stronger than the rest, a little more in control. And as he looked over at Vuong and Wilkes, he felt a little more of his fear slip away.

On the bridge, Baker sat quietly, his hands clasped firmly to the armrests of his seat. He knew that Portofino was one of the best pilots the military had to offer, and that there was no way she would ever allow her bird to go down, but as the vessel began to shake against the pounding air outside, he found himself having to convince himself even more of that fact. He could feel his stomach boiling inside his gut, his greasy, bile-filled intestines twisting around each other as the ship lurched back and forth. He pressed his eyes closed, forcing everything to turn black, until all but the deep rumble of the ship's engines surrounded him.

The turbulence increased, and the sound of metal being stressed to bend punched through the darkness Baker was hiding in, pounding relentlessly against his eyelids, shaking him violently in an attempt to get him to open them, for him to see the last horrifying seconds before the ship plunged headlong into the ground, killing them all in a scorching ball of twisted metal and flame. But he maintained his silent composure, his hands clasped together in his lap, eyelids pressed tight. Then, as he was sure they were moments away from impact, the shaking calmed and Portofino's voice filled his ears.

"All clear, we're green across the board."

Baker exhaled, a shuddered breath silently escaping his lips, and then he slowly allowed his eyes to open. On the view screen was a vast landscape of orange and red, a blended palate of titian Earth as far as the image spanned. He stared at the planet's surface slipping past beneath and felt the cool sweat of relief dripping down his back beneath his shirt. His fingers were cramped, and he realized that they were still interlocked so tightly in his lap that the thin webs of flesh between them threatened to tear. Slowly he released his grip, pulling them apart and wiping the cold clamminess on his fatigues.

"Switching to thermal."

Portofino hit a switch on the console and the image in front of them morphed into a 3D texture map of the planet moving past below. A sea of blue, red and green filled the screen as she navigated closer to the surface. Once the shaking stopped, she switched back to standard vision and the desolate, red face of the planet fell back into view.

Baker watched as the endless sea of burnt hue continued to move past, admiring how similar it looked up close on the vid screen as it did in the pictures he'd seen back home, when Talmadge spoke up from behind him.

"There she is." There was a pride in his voice as he spoke, a parent on teacher day as their child receives the outstanding student award. "Sixty billion dollars right there, and the next step in humanity."

Baker watched as the dot on the distant horizon began to grow closer.

"There's nothing like it in the galaxy—the first of its kind, hands down the greatest thing ever created by man, and the most challenging."

The speck turned into a mass, and the mass formed into structures, an entire facility growing before his eyes as they approached.

"Guess they should have spent a little more of that budget on communications..."

This time Baker stifled his grin as Wilkes' words drew a stop to Talmadge's bragging. Hell, he almost wanted to congratulate him for thinking so quickly.

Portofino slowed the ship down, the blur beneath them forming into shapes as individual rocks and hills began to form across the surface. The facility now stood in full view, a massive structure of titanium and steel, contrasting against the Earth that surrounded it.

"Approach vector, six one nine. Coming in slow and low."

Baker stared at the structure. He had seen pictures of the facility, diagrams drawn by computers that showed the station shining brightly against the perfect Mars  backdrop, the sun glinting beautifully off the polished surface. But as they approached it, he saw that the outer walls were tarnished from the harsh conditions of the planet, sub-zero temperatures that dropped hundreds of degrees below zero dulling the exterior to a matte finish. There were two main sections branched off of the main facility, and as they drew nearer he could see a large bay with two massive sliding doors shut tightly, a well-worn path leading outwards, disappearing into the desolate wasteland. He scanned for movement, his eyes straining to pick up any signs of activity. But as the ship closed in, the only thing that greeted them was the silent curves of the Attis Station.

"Let's give it a sweep," Baker said, continuing to scan the colony as it grew to take up nearly all of the screen.

"Roger that, swinging around for visual."

Portofino dropped the ship lower and pulled back on the throttle, swinging it in a slow arc.

As they circled, Baker was reminded of the research facilities he'd seen once in a magazine about the Antarctic before it had nearly melted away. There were dozens of buildings, all white, rounded at the top, and connected by arched tunnels. The entire facility was compacted, with an oversized landing site in the front and a massive steel and titanium platform at the rear.

"That's the mining bay," Talmadge said as they circled around the back.

"How many people did you say were stationed here?" he asked, his gaze scanning the dark windows along the structures.

"We have thirty-five families at this facility: scientists and miners mostly. There's a medical crew, security detail and a branch of our corporate office just to maintain the administrative detail. We're planning on having it expanded enough within the next two years to allow for another forty to fifty families. We're building a school and we have a state of the art hydroponics facility that's almost complete. By the end of the year, they'll be fully self-sustained."

Baker stared at the facility moving past as they circled around. The knot tightened. There were no lights, no movement. It seemed derelict; dead. A cold foreboding slowly began to chip into him, the feelings he had felt when watching the woman on the vid screen rekindling in his gut. He continued scanning the building, taking note of the darkened windows and still platforms. "With that many people and mining operations running, I would have thought we'd arrive to a larger welcoming committee." There was nothing. "Wilkes, run a biometric scan of the facility. Let's find out where the hell all the people are and why we're not getting a response."

Wilkes pulled a cable from the console next to him and plugged it into his holowrist. "Initiating scan now."

Baker continued to watch the structure, looking for obvious signs of breach or struggle. The facility was in perfect condition, not a mark on it. It was just dark; no outside lights, no light coming from the interior, nothing. It was as silent as the space that surrounded them before they arrived.

"That's strange," Wilkes said after a moment.
"What is it?" Baker asked, a hollow feeling working into his chest.

"I'm not getting any readings Sarge. It's dark in there."
"That's not possible," Talmadge said, leaning forward in his chair to get a closer look at the viewscreen. "We had active transmissions with the colony just three weeks ago."

"It's space," Baker responded flatly. "Anything could have happened, and no one would find out until they came looking." He paused, turning to look at the rep. "You said this was a prototype, right—the first of its kind? Any number of things could have happened that your company didn't account for until it was attempted in the field." He struggled to find a polite way to dance semantically around what he was truly feeling. The station was dead, he could feel it. Behind him Talmadge continued to rattle on.

"We ran every diagnostic scan and hypothetical algorithm possible before we started construction. We had the best engineers on Earth design this facility, and the best contractors on the planet overseeing its construction. We ran so many simulations we even had algorithms running algorithms just to create probable disaster." Baker's accusation had burrowed deep into the man's skin. He was assaulting the integrity of the company, and questioning its abilities. This was one of the things that stabbed him the deepest. He loved the company, rallied by everything it stood for, and would die a company man. Xenocorp was the best thing to happen to the galaxy. The sergeant was a stupid grunt and had no place speaking about things he didn't understand. No place. "There is nothing short of an asteroid impacting directly into this facility that could cause it to go black."

"Maybe everybody just took a vacation," Wilkes said from behind.

This time Baker didn't smile, but he didn't jump to reprimand him either. The others could sense that something had gone wrong, that the darkness coming from the facility was far beyond what the simulations had prepared for.

"Alright, Portofino, let's set her down."

The front of the facility came into view again, with the landing pad a short distance away. As they approached, Baker took notice of the two rovers parked just off to the side. *If someone wanted to leave, those'd be the way to go...* Again, something didn't sit right with him. "Nice and easy-like. And I want full view of the doors before we shut her down."

"Roger that. Bringing her down nice and easy."

The ship touched down with a small shudder, the landing gear clanking heavy to the steel platform below. There was a loud hiss as the engine purged the heat from the exhaust. Portofino flicked a row of switches and the dim red lighting inside the ship turned green for a second, then illuminated white again.

"Alright, marines," Baker said, bringing the comms up. "We're going in live. I want a standard dismount with exit by the numbers. Fascio, Vuong. You two take point. I want that hatch opened ricky-fuckin-tick. Wilkes, give me one more bioscan, and Portofino, you stay here and keep her warm. I'd like to be back space-side before breakfast peaks."

"Roger that."

Replies came in single file.

In the personnel hold, the rest of the marines began suiting up. They slipped tactical vests over their uniforms, followed by a thick belt that housed their envirosuit. One by one they checked each other's equipment, and when they were finished, they engaged the small button on their belt pack that pushed a thin protective suit out from the back.

With practiced precision each of the soldiers slipped their arms and legs into the nano-fiber and sealed it in the front. They did one last check for seal leaks on their face masks and then made their way to the cargo bay. By the time they finished, they looked the part of a tactical marine unit they had been hired to be.

It was moments later that the Sarge, Wilkes, and Talmadge entered the bay.

"All right, ladies. Let's keep it quick; I've got a lunch date with cryo."

Wilkes reached up and hit the button above the doorway, and there was a loud whoosh of air as the atmosphere outside sucked out the oxygen in a rush. The group stepped onto the platform and made their way towards the facility.

As they stepped closer, Corlin clicked in. "Sarge, it doesn't look like anybody's home."

Baker had the same feeling creeping up his spine.
"Just keep it by the books, Corporal."
The wind was almost nonexistent; an invisible breeze blocked by their envirosuits. They knew the air around them was freezing, but the thermal regulators in their suits didn't allow for them to notice; only the temp on their heads-up display told them it was negative fifty degrees with oxygen levels almost nonexistent.

Baker pressed forward, his eyes scanning the sprawling facility acutely. Instinctively he checked every corner, every dark space, every nook. As he approached the dual doors leading to the outer airlock, he slowed, motioning for the two marines behind him to move forward.

Fascio made his way past him and reached the door, where Vuong immediately began working on the exterior console. Fascio stood alert with his rifle poised at the ground near his feet.

"How's it coming?" Fascio asked as the others approached.

"Like your mother every time I go home."

Fascio smiled beneath his helm. "You know, I'm gonna be pretty pissed if we get in there and find out we came all this way because some dumbass colonist hit the mute button..."

"Well," Vuong replied, glancing with a smile. "We'll find out soon enough won't we?"

He pressed two wires together and the doors moved to the side with a loud groan.

"On the ready," Baker said as he approached with the rest. "Last thing we want is a firefight because we spooked their security team."

As they entered the main airlock, an uneasiness worked through the unit. There was no personnel to greet them, no lights, nothing. It seemed as if the facility had been completely abandoned.

"Patch in, Vuong," Baker said as he stepped into the outer hatch. "I want a full report before we breach. Let me know what we're walking into."

The other nodded, moving quickly to the inner door and using a small tool to open a panel just beside it. A moment later he turned his head to look at him. "Sarge," Vuong said as the door sealed behind them. "Environmental regulators are offline..."

"That's impossible," Talmadge barked across the comms before the soldier could finish telling them what it meant. "Our environmental system is completely automated. It's designed to run for the next thousand years. There's no way it could fail. We have failsafes to guard the failsafes. They have to be turned off manually, and the only person with authorization codes to do that is the director."

"Well, by all means," Vuong replied, shooting an exasperated look to the company man, "Feel free to take off your mask if you don't believe me."

"That's enough, Vuong," Baker interjected flatly. "Just get that inner door open and then we'll figure out what the hell's going on once we're inside."

"Roger that, Sarge."

Baker looked at the others as Vuong moved to the next door panel. The cold around him seemed to seep into his suit, his skin clamping tightly against muscle and bone. He tapped his holowrist and opened a private comms channel. "What do you think, Wilkes? What the hell's happened here?"

"I don't know, Sarge, but if I had to guess, this place went ass-over-tits, and I have a feeling that the suit is here as damage control. One thing I do know, is that with environmental offline, unless they had a rather large supply of breathing units on hand, I don't think we're gonna find anything good in there."

"We're in," Vuong said, cracking across the comms.

"All right. Then let's see what we got waiting for us."

Baker signaled Corlin and Fascio to the doors. They slung their rifles to the back and grabbed the doors at the center, pulling them back as fast as the frozen steel would allow.

"Holy shit!!!"

Fascio jumped back, his rifle flinging into his hands as he pulled off three rounds into the lifeless corpses that fell outwards as the door parted. Corlin stepped backwards as well, his hand quickly bringing his pistol to bear.

"Cease fire goddamnit!" Baker yelled. "Cease fire!"

The entire unit acted as one, every rifle leveling at the half-opened doors and the two bodies that had fallen through the cracked entrance.

"Jesus Christ…" Fascio spat.

"Stay sharp, marines," Baker said, his own hand moving to his sidearm. "Get those doors the rest of the way open and let's get some light in there. And Fascio, you pull that shit again, you'll be walking back to Earth."

Fascio shot a worried glance at Corlin and they moved back into place, pushing the doors the rest of the way open.

Baker stared down at the bodies. No blood. Fascio had just fired three rounds into the corpses and there wasn't so much as a splatter. Tiny shards of frozen, cloth covered flesh had exploded outwards, shimmering on the floor against the invading sunlight. He realized at that moment that their systems had been offline long enough for the outside temperature to press its way inside, freezing steel and flesh alike.

"What the fuck...?"

Corlin's light came up and splashed across the scene before them. Just inside the corridor was a handful of bodies. There was crimson shimmering across the walls and the floor was a massive puddle of crystal burgundy; blood frozen into a sheet of ice.

Baker moved into the corridor, Corlin, Wilkes, and Fascio immediately behind him. Behind that, the rest of the crew made their way nervously into the hall of death.

"What the hell happened here, Lanskey," Baker asked, struggling to hold his voice steady as his eyes took in the slaughtered corpses spread from one end to the other.

Lanskey approached the first of the bodies and bent to inspect them. Moments passed by like days.

"I... I don't know how else to put this Sarge, but it looks like someone took an axe to these people. We've got multiple lacerations, some so deep they severed bone. From the markings on these ones, a quick evaluation says from the nature of the wounds, these folks died defending themselves. Most of the lacerations classify as defensive, having occurred on the hands and forearms, and the bodies in the front sustained most of their injuries to the back." She paused, looking up to Baker. "Sarge... These people were slaughtered."

His chest tightened and he could feel the sweat beginning to seep across his brow beneath the fiber wrapped helm.

*"I have to get to the director's office."*

Baker broke his gaze with Lanskey and moved it to Talmadge who stood, eyes wide and fists clenched to a ball. "I need to get there now."

Baker took a deep breath, steadying himself for his reply. He stared in disbelief at the weaselly rep, seconds ticking away as he decided how to properly form his reply, remembering that everything he said could be stored for use against him upon return. "I think we have a whole list of other things that have just taken priority over you checking your company's financials." Anger began to build. Their trip had just taken a turn for the longer, and as it stood before them, the entire facility had taken to ending up dead. He was appalled by the fact that the first thing the rep was concerned with was making sure the company wasn't going to be held liable for the deaths of the thirty-five families they had brought there. The anger began to border on disbelief. In a flash he no longer cared what the rep thought, or what he would do when they got back.

"Look, I need—"

"What you need to do, is shut the hell up and let me figure out just what the hell we're supposed to do now," Baker interrupted. "It seems obvious to me, that some pretty serious shit's gone down here, and the last thing I'm going to do, is put my men in jeopardy so that you can take a little field trip. We have no idea if who, or what it was that caused all this, isn't still roaming around the facility waiting for more people to arrive, so that they can continue what it seems to me, they already started. So do me a favor, and shut the hell up for a minute."

Talmadge held his tongue, fury coursing through him as he turned away and walked to the back of the group. The soldier had apparently forgotten his position on the ladder, but at this moment, his focus was on retrieving the data that had been collected, and sealing off any information that could be detrimental to the company's image. Things had to appear as though everything had gone by the numbers, and that it was simply an isolated incident, caused by a miscalculation in the psych department back home.

Someone had given them false information prior to screening, and had laid a well-orchestrated lie in order to get themselves hired on at the colony for the sole purpose of sabotage. The wheels had already started turning, well oiled, corporate cogs quickly spinning the gears in his mind as he created elaborate scenarios.

"Fascio, you take point. Dom, Corlin, on his six. Let's go see what the hell's happened to the rest of these fine folks."

Fascio nodded to Dom who moved quickly to the front, followed by Corlin.

"And I think it's safe to say, safeties off."

Baker let the others move past, but stopped Talmadge as he attempted to move past him. He opened a private channel and held the rep's arm as he spoke.

"Look, Talmadge. It's obvious that you don't like me, and to be honest, I don't care. I myself, can't stand corporate, bureaucratic rats, and you just so happen to stink like one. But since we didn't come all this way to become friends, I really feel as though we should focus on the situation at hand. I understand that it was your company that paid for this little trip, and that it's your best interests at hand, but at the moment, it appears that something a little bigger than our own petty likes has occurred here. So, I suggest we get really good at working with each other, because that's the only way this is going to work. On the way here, it was your game, but this..." Baker swept his hand towards the corpses on the floor. "This is mine, and I happen to be very good at it. So, I suggest we worry about what's happened, versus what will." He paused as the rep stared back at him with gritted teeth behind the clear visor. "Now, I'll get you to your director's office, but first, we need to worry about our immediate situation. We need to get environmental back online, cause these tanks we're breathing out of, they aren't bottomless, and when they run out... Well let's just say that'll make for a very short trip. And after that, we need to see what it was that caused this, incident, which means we need to get to security. Once I've secured our current situation, I'll make sure you get escorted to your office. Now, is that okay with you?"

Talmadge stared at him with hatred burning behind his gaze, but he knew the soldier was right. Something had happened, and whatever it was, was going to cost a lot of money, and possibly a good amount of reputation for the company. He needed to tread very carefully. He needed to ensure as little of this made it out as possible. The soldiers were shackled under strict nondisclosure contracts, but what he was truly worried about was that one of the colonists managed to get something out to the public before communications went down, and the only way he would know that, is if he read through the director's files, which meant at this moment, he had to play the game, and that was what he was good at.

46

Talmadge nodded. "Sure. Yeah. Your game."

Baker let the man's arm go and nodded. "Good. Now where might we find environmental?"

6

Shadows writhed along the corridor walls, slithering into every crevice and corner as the unit pressed deeper into the heart of the abandoned facility. Fascio led the way, his rifle's beam slicing through the suffocating black—a stark, visceral trail of blood splattered across corrugated steel, gleaming wetly beneath the trembling light. The air was thick with the metallic tang of old violence, so dense it seemed to seep through their suits, clinging to their skin like a cold, damp shroud. Each step disturbed scattered boxes, remnants of a desperate flight, their contents spilled in frantic abandon. Every surface shimmered with a sickly sheen as the flashlight swept ahead, but beyond the reach of their lights, the darkness pressed in, heavy and absolute. The only sound was the echo of their own footsteps, swallowed by an eerie, predatory silence.

Baker's nerves screamed for night vision, the absence of tactical helmets gnawing at his composure. The blackness felt alive, a sentient void that watched and waited. He forced himself to focus, to make do with what little protection they had, but every instinct told him they were exposed—vulnerable.

Twenty meters in, Fascio's light froze on a single, smeared handprint—dark burgundy, fingers splayed in terror—dragged down the wall and vanishing into the gloom ahead. "What the hell happened here, Sarge?" Fascio whispered, his voice barely more than a breath, the comms crackling with unease.

Baker didn't answer immediately, his heart hammering as he cursed himself for flinching. Whatever had happened here, he was certain none of them wanted to know. "Wilkes, can you get auxiliary power up?" he murmured, voice tight.

"It depends on the extent of the damage. I'll check the next panel we come across and run diagnostics. Should be able to reroute power from somewhere," Wilkes replied, but even his words sounded hollow, swallowed by the oppressive dark.

Baker's gaze dropped to a frosted puddle of blood on the floor, footprints trailing away into the corridor's depths. The dread was suffocating, a claustrophobic pressure that seemed to squeeze the air from their lungs as they moved forward, each step heavier than the last.

"Sarge," Fascio hissed, "one o'clock."

Baker followed the trembling beam to a grotesque tableau: three bodies huddled against a metal crate, limbs twisted and fused by the cold, frozen flesh merging one corpse into another. The sight clawed at his mind, a twitch jerking at his eye as sweat prickled beneath his suit's internal regulator. He longed for a cigarette—anything to anchor him to normalcy—but all he could do was stare.

"Lanskey," he managed, voice raw, eyes locked on the dead colonists.

The medical officer stepped forward, her penlight trembling as she illuminated the crystallized mass. Blood and frozen flesh sparkled beneath the crimson-stained cloth, the horror of the scene revealed in stark, merciless detail.

"It's the same thing, Sarge," she said after a moment. As she spoke, she noticed that two of the bodies had blades still frozen in their grasp. She reached down, inspecting the weapons closer, and then startled softly at the realization. "It looks like these people did this to each other."

Baker stepped closer, stopping just behind her.

She pointed to a woman slumped against the wall. "The wounds on her neck and chest are consistent with the knife in that one's hand." She moved her light to a younger man who was sprawled on the floor at the woman's feet. "And the puncture marks across his left cheek match the screwdriver she's holding." She paused, her gaze lifting to meet Baker's. "These people killed each other. I'd say an altercation is an understatement of what happened here."

"What the fuck..." Corlin moved his light away, sending the beam trailing further down the hallway. "I don't like this, Sarge. Not at all. This is fubar." He wasn't a stranger to seeing things like this. He'd been at the front lines in Rwanda and had witnessed firsthand the things capable during war at the hands of the warring tribes. But there was something about this that wormed its way under his skin and continued to crawl beneath the surface. Maybe it was the way that everyone had simply disappeared, or that without the help of environmental controls, everything was frozen, perfectly preserved carnage in full grotesqueness, saved for them to stumble across in its full, macabre glory.

"Let's just get to environmental," Baker replied. "We need to get these systems back online. Maybe then, we can make our way to security and figure out what the hell went on in here. Until then, Marine, I need us to keep it together."

Corlin swallowed hard. He was visibly shaken and as Baker looked into his eyes he could see that he was on the border of panic. He was the largest man in his unit, six foot three and two hundred and twenty pounds, pure hardened muscle strapped to a solid steel frame, and Baker had been in more than his fair share of situations with him that neither of them thought they were getting out of alive. But there and then, as he stared into the other's eyes, he saw something he had never seen before: fear, very real, and completely unhidden.

"Let's keep moving," Baker said, still holding eye contact with the big man. "Talmadge, how much farther?"

"Not far."
"Then lead the way."

Baker didn't trust Talmadge. Nothing about him sat right with him. He could feel ulterior motive oozing from the rep as he moved past. He waited until he was a few feet ahead and clicked Vuong on a private channel. "Vuong, could you pull up a schematic of the facility? I'd like to know where we're going in here."

"Roger that," Vuong replied, tapping his holowrist to life and working his fingers quickly across the keyboard. A minute later a holographic projection of the facility popped up in front of them. "There you go. We're here, and environmental's *here*."

"Copy that," Baker replied, turning to follow the others.

The first room they came to was admissions. The door leading in was propped open, a pipe wedged into the floor holding it inside the wall. Fascio could see blood splatter along the floor and wall even before he reached it. He knew without looking what horrors waited him inside.

"Every person that comes to the facility has to go through admissions," Talmadge said, pulling Baker's attention from the soldier that stood staring blankly into the open room. "They're processed and logged, given their ID number and clearance. We managed to streamline the process so..."

Baker couldn't believe what he was hearing. The company weasel was still talking about his station with pride, as if giving them the grand tour to their brand new facility on opening day. They had just walked past the product of his creation, death the kind only told in books and movies back home, and that asshole was still standing there like a real estate agent pitching a beach front house. Something in his eyes must have clued the other in and he immediately changed direction.

"Environmental's down the hall on the right," Talmadge said, his gaze glancing nervously to the floor and back.

"Sarge."

Baker turned to Wilkes who had his light pinned to the back of the room.

"There's an access panel. I may be able to reroute power from here."

"Do it. Fascio, Dom, post security. If anything so much as blinks in this hallway, you put it down."

The men moved past him as Wilkes made his way into the room, sweeping the corners with his light as he moved to the electrical panel. Around him, darkness pressed in, the scene behind it hidden away beyond a veil of black. He opened the panel and ran a cable from the display to his holowrist. A second later the display illuminated. Behind him, Baker stood at the doorway, his eyes straining to see through the endless pitch of the hallway. Part of him hoped the lights wouldn't come back on. If the rest of the facility was anything like what they'd seen already, then it wasn't something he wanted to see. Again, his thoughts went to the night vision he was used to having.

"Got it," Wilkes said, his voice cracking across the comms as a thin flicker of light began to illuminate through the slotted grates that comprised the walls.

Baker steeled himself for what he knew was coming.

Overhead, the emergency lights slowly came to light, peeling back the cover that held the rest of the horror at bay. Light slowly filtered through the hallway, unmasking the violence that had stayed hidden in the dark. From one end of the hall to the other, paper and boxes were scattered, bloodstained remnants of colonists scrambling desperately to escape. Containers were overturned and articles from the colonist's lives lay scattered from one end to the other. Baker felt his stomach knot as the reality of the situation came to full bare. Whatever had happened here had happened quickly, and no one had a chance. The frigid unease burrowed deeper.

Inside the room the overhead lights cast their glow across the surface. "My god," Wilkes whispered, his gaze falling to the wall in front of him. "Sarge. Might wanna see this."

Baker felt his skin flex tight as Wilkes' words pressed into his ears. He turned and made his way into the room where he was standing, his gaze locked to the wall in front of him. Written across the wall was a single sentence. *Don't believe the whispers.* He read it, every word punching home, realizing at the same time the medium in which it was painted in. The knot in his stomach tightened. "This just keeps getting better." He turned and made his way back into the hall, glancing through the thin beams of light that illuminated outwards from the wall panels. Above were inset lights every twenty feet that cast a shadow through the haze of particles hanging in the air. With no atmosphere the image looked like a grainy, still framed photograph. He shifted, glancing past Fascio to where the corridor curved out of view. The feeling of unseen eyes peering back at him burrowed into him and he found himself staring back, waiting for the hidden monstrosity to appear as he turned the scrawled words over and over again in his mind. What the hell did that mean? And what whispers..?

"All right marines, let's move," he said after a moment, the command coming out barely past a nervous exhale.

The rest of the hallway was the same, personal effects scattered along the floor, blood splatter on the walls and dried puddles glistening on the floor as the dim light cast across their icy surface. Baker wrestled with the sight, clinging desperately to the hope that they would find some rational explanation for it all; a system malfunction or colonist gone off the deep end, but every stain he passed, every name badge lying cast away at his feet, pushed that thought further and further away. Whatever happened here had happened fast, and had not been contained.

The group continued onward, reaching a section where the corridor branched off ten minutes later. The signs along the ceiling that were now illuminated in dull green read, *Administration*, with a small arrow pointing to the left and *Central Housing* to the right. Baker looked to Vuong who nodded silently to another sign on the ceiling that read *Environmental*. Talmadge walked up and began to tell them it was just ahead when Baker cut him off. "I know, I can read." He wasn't in the mood for more braggadocio about the corpse installation.

The hallway leading past environmental to central housing was at a slight incline. He made his way up, stopping a short distance from the closed hatch as the others came to a halt behind. He took a deep breath and held it in his chest.

"Fascio, Dom, Wilkes, Corlin, stack up. I want a clean entry. No surprises."

The men moved to the door, two on each side and nodded to each other. Corlin, who was at the rear, reached out and patted Wilkes from behind, the others doing the same. At the same time Fascio reached out and pressed the switch on the wall. As the door opened with a soft whoosh, Dom charged inside, his rifle at the ready. The others followed immediately behind him, their lights sweeping the room in a matter of seconds. "Clear."

Baker stepped into the room and surveyed the scene. Though environmental wasn't online, and there was no way anyone could have survived this long in a zero oxygen atmosphere, he still expected some monster or crazed maniac to jump out at him. It was his nature to be cautious. It was his job.

Along one wall were a series of computer monitors. They were all blank, one of them cracked across the front where it looked as if someone had hit it with something heavy. The chairs in front of them were strewn about and the cabling along the back wall had been torn free and cut multiple times. Colorful cabling twisted outwards like the frayed ends of a weathered sweater. As Baker made his way into the room he exhaled deeply, relieved that it was the first room they entered that hadn't looked like a crime scene. "Vuong, start earning that pay."

Vuong nodded, examining the monitors and moving to the cables. "Well good news is the cables here, they were just for the monitoring station. Environmental controls are in the room back there." He nodded to another door at the back to the L-shaped room.

"Corlin, pie that room."

The marine turned and made his way to the door, pressing the button and standing ready as the door slid to the side. As it opened, and the lights came to life, he twitched to move forward and then stopped in his tracks. He instantly flinched backwards, staggering backward two steps before leaning to the side and vomiting heavily into his helmet.

Dom stepped forward quickly as the vacuum pump in Corlin's suit immediately purged the puke from within and misted the inside of his visor. "Jesus Christ," he whispered, the color flushing from his face as the sight before him came into view. Behind them, Baker tensed.

Seated in a chair facing the door was a man in a clean cut suit, the Xenocorp logo embroidered neatly on the lapel. His face was a visceral honeycomb of deep gashes and cuts, skin flayed outwards. Everything from his neck down was completely covered in a frosted layer of coagulated blood, and there was a large pool that had worked its way outwards, stretching towards the door, suspended by the sub-zero chill. Hanging loosely from one hand was a pair of gore-covered scissors. Dom found himself thankful for a moment that environmental was still offline. He shuddered at the thought of the smell they would have unleashed when the door opened, and what three weeks of rot would have looked like.

Baker pushed Dom aside, allowing the sight before him to hit him full force. He felt the muscles in the back of his neck tighten and felt a ripple crawl across his skin. "Lanskey, please tell me you have an explanation for this." The chief medical officer made her way to the room, pausing as she reached the door. One hand came up to her mouth and she turned her gaze to the floor just outside as she composed herself. After a deep breath she stepped inside and leaned in to examine the body. "Severe lacerations and puncture wounds to the neck and face. Repeated stabbing." She paused, turning to face the sergeant. "Sergeant...."

Baker nodded, not needing her to finish her diagnosis. The man in the chair had committed suicide in a way he struggled to find possible; by stabbing himself in the face repeatedly until his life had drained to the floor beneath him. Both of his eyes were punctured to the point of complete absence, and there were multiple holes in his gums and cheeks. He had severed the skin across his forehead so bad that a large flap folded down past what remained of his blood-matted eyebrows. Baker struggled to rationalize how someone could wrench past their body's own defense mechanism, pushing beyond the limits one's mind would allow. It should have been physically impossible for someone to inflict that much harm to themselves. The man's system should have gone into shock after the first couple of blows, but the corpse in front of him had continued, again and again until only death forced his hand to stop.

"Hawkes," Baker said softly, wrenching his gaze from the body in the chair. "Find something to cover this poor bastard."

*"That's the director."*

Baker jerked his head around to see Talmadge standing directly behind him, his face blank, no emotion to be read behind the paled skin.

"Well, I suppose that took care of the password problem," he responded flatly, turning to push past Talmadge into the room, making sure the impact of his shoulder knocked him off balance. He had hoped this trip would be short, routine. He'd been looking forward to getting back to Earth and setting his affairs into order. He had gladly taken this assignment, knowing it would give him just enough time to sort his thoughts before going back to the reality that waited for him. Now, as he made his way past the unit that stood silently in the room, he knew their trip was going to be a lot longer than they had all expected.

Moments later Hawkes reappeared, a light grey tarp in his hand.

"Vuong, see if you can get us up and running will you," Baker said, his jaw clenched tightly in his helmet.

"Roger that, Sarge," he replied, waiting for Hawkes to make his way back out with the wrapped corpse before entering the control room.

The sergeant took a deep breath, exhaling long and slow. Then he made his way to Corlin who was sitting with his back to the wall, arms hanging loosely over his knees. "You okay?" he asked, already knowing, there was no way he could be. None of them could.

"Yeah, Sarge. Just wasn't expecting that. Wasn't expecting any of this." His gaze moved up to meet his commander's. "This isn't what we signed up for. Something really bad's happened here, and I know I'm not supposed to be. We're not allowed. But I'm scared." Baker stared down at the man for a moment before replying, a response he wasn't expecting coming out. "Me too. None of this is right. And I just wanna figure out what the hell has happened, clear any threat, and hightail it back to Earth as soon as we can. And trust me, I'm gonna put in for an extended leave for all of us once we get back Earthside."

Corlin nodded, his gaze moving back to the floor. "I'll be all right, Sarge, I just need a minute."

Baker nodded, the only compassionate thing he could do. "Okay. We got this."

"Sarge?"

Baker turned to see Lanskey approaching him.

"I think I should get to medical. There might be something in the logs that can help us figure out what the hell has happened here. Something had to have been reported before all of this occurred; some, I don't know, symptoms. We need to know if this is a pathogen, or viral. We can't risk bringing whatever this is back, which means, before we can leave, we need to know what it is." Baker nodded, glancing to the other men in the room. Her words wrapped his mind in a thick film. Before we can leave... "As soon as Vuong gets environmental back online, we should get to communications. We need to send a sit-rep to command and let them know the clusterfuck that's happened here. Then I agree, there must be something in medical. If it's some type of virus, then as much as I hate the fact that I'm about to say these words, I have to agree with you, we can't risk bringing anything back to Earth with us."

A loud hiss filled the room as plumes of mist billowed from the overhead vents, swirling the icy dust hanging in the air wildly. "Got it!"

Vuong exclaimed from the room, stepping out a moment later as the facility began the process of purging the air and replacing it with a breathable atmosphere.

"How long till we're green?" Baker asked, already seeing the temperature rise in his HUD.

"Twenty, thirty max till we're at safe levels."

"Good." Baker turned. "Wilkes, I want this room sealed. No one comes in or out. I want you to seal her up tighter than a Mormon girl on prom night, you hear me?"

"Roger that."

"Vuong, how far to comms?"

"Back the way we came, end of the second hallway."

"Alright then. Let's wrap this up."

The group moved into the hallway, followed by Wilkes who turned and fired up a small ion torch he had pulled from a pack on his belt. He immediately began welding the doorframe, double welding along the seams. Baker watched as blue and white sparks fell to the floor beneath. His thoughts shifted to medical, and he could feel the sweat beading across his brow as he wrestled with what they would do if it was in fact something communicable. He knew the events that would unfold in that scenario and they were a long list of things that would keep him from getting home; quarantine, followed by weeks of observation, followed by psych exams and then more testing. It would be weeks until he was able to return, and all that time would be stuck at the derelict station, surrounded by the shadow of death. When Wilkes was finished, he pulled his sidearm and fired two rounds into the door panel. "Just an added preventative," he said, turning to nod at Baker.

"All right. Let's move out."

7

The air in the facility had begun to circulate, the particles that had hung stationary in the air now gone, replaced by a thin haze of atmosphere that slowly spread through the hallways. The unit walked in silence, each of them stepping with frayed nerves as they doubled back. They passed the intersection that led back to the landing pad, following the sign that read *Communications*. As they made their way to the end of the hall, Baker saw an illuminated poster on the wall. As he passed, he saw a group of smiling factory workers, clean clothes and a perfectly placed smudge of oil on their cheeks. Above it, read *Xenocorp, better planets for all*. "Not these poor bastards," he scoffed to himself, pausing as he read the words, *THEY LIE,* scrawled across the wall just below it. He realized the irony of it as he made his way past, following just behind Dom and Hawkes.

"Better planets...?"
Baker shook his head as Mills approached from behind.

"You think they'd have started by building a decent facility," Mills added.

Baker clicked his tongue against the roof of his mouth. "You read that too huh?"

"Yeah," Mills replied, shifting the rifle strap across his chest. "Guessing they have some type of protocol for when shit like this happens."

"Shit like this doesn't just happen. There's something else going on, and I can't shake the feeling we just haven't found it yet."

Ahead, Dom and Hawkes had reached the end of the corridor. Vuong approached the open door and stopped, staring for a moment before turning to look down the hall at them and cracking across the comms. "I think this might take a minute."

Baker approached, stopping at the doorway. Inside the room was a series of control consoles along the walls, chairs cast aside carelessly. The main console against the back wall was completely destroyed, wires and metal twisting outwards, a shimmering pile of shattered computer components below. Someone had made short work of the equipment, ensuring whoever came after, would have a hell of a time trying to get any messages out.

Vuong stepped into the room and stopped, his hand raising to the top of his head. "Jesus. Looks like somebody took a sledgehammer to it." He paused, turning around to look at Sarge. "One thing for sure, we won't be making any long distance calls."

"Can you get it working?" Baker asked, knowing the answer before he even formed the words, but hope forcing them out.

65

Vuong shook his head. "It's dead, Sarge. Whoever did this, made damn sure nobody was going to be sending any outgoing messages any time soon."

"Shit."

Baker brought his hands up to his mask and rubbed his cheeks. "Portofino, I need you to send a distress call. Tell command that our situation is compromised and that we need backup sent here immediately. Tell them we have a code twelve and there's no salvage. I want that message sent on the double."

*"Sergeant!"*

Baker turned to see Talmadge standing at the back of the group.

"I can't authorize that. You're under strict nondisclosure. Anything that goes out needs to be read and approved by myself, and I cannot allow you to send that message."

Baker started forward, his hands balling to fists. "You listen here you son of a bitch. Do you not see what the fuck is happening here?" All protocol was off. He could feel the fury boiling in a torrent in his veins. The facility, the death, everything disappeared behind the rage that erupted in him. "Your little social experiment has gone and fucked itself inside out. Everyone here is dead!" He stopped, his mask inches away from Talmadge's. "Now, I don't give two shits what you think you authorize. You and your company can kiss my ass. These folks are dead, and I'll be God damned if I'm gonna let them

66

stay here and rot so your company can cover its ass, nor will I stay here to join them. So, stay the fuck out of my way and keep your god damn mouth shut." Baker could feel his arms trembling. It had been a long time since he'd had to fight the urge to pound someone in the ground that bad. He wanted to beat him within an inch of his life, but he held his composure. He had a full unit of marines that were on the border of losing it, and if he faltered, then there would be no one to hold them together. That was the only thing that kept Talmadge from returning to the ship on a stretcher. "Portofino, do you read me?"

Baker stood with his mask three inches away from Talmadge's. He didn't blink, he didn't flinch, he just held his gaze, staring deep into the portals beyond his soul. He wanted him to know his command had been taken, wanted everyone to see the company rat back down. He knew his unit would follow him to a full court-martial with no hesitation, but he wanted to make it crystal clear to the other. "Portofino?"

Talmadge unclenched his teeth, the coppery taste of blood slowly filling his mouth where they had pushed deep into his gums. He knew there was nothing he could do at that moment. He had lost, but once they got back to Earth, or he found communications, he would have that man's career. He had worked for the company for twenty-five years, and not once had anyone ever spoken to him like that. No one in that unit knew what he was capable of; or the friends he had and the positions they held. Sergeant Williams had taken his last patrol, and by the time he was done with him, he'd be lucky to land a job scrubbing toilets in a fast food restaurant. With a scoff he turned around and pressed his back against the wall. He could see the condensation building around them as the temperature rose, pushing the layer of ice crystals back, the atmosphere slowly building in the facility.

"God damnit," Baker spat, turning to his unit. "Corlin, Hawkes, get your asses back to the ship on the double. I wanna know why Portofino's not responding. When you get there, you send a message to HQ and tell them in the nicest way possible, that things have gone ass over tits down here. And I want the two of you back before I have time to even notice you were gone. Do you copy?"

"Yes, Sir."

"Come on," Corlin said, tapping Hawkes in the chest.

The pair turned and made their way quickly down the hall, disappearing around the turn a short distance ahead.

"Vuong, where's security?"

"Back the way we came, just past environmental."

"I'm getting about sick and tired of this back and forth shit," Baker growled.

"I need to get to the director's office," Talmadge sneered, his back still pressed into the wall.

"Does it look like I give a fuck about what you think you need, Talmadge?"

The rep's face scrunched to a knot as bitter anger warped his features.

"Dom, you take Lanskey and head to Medical. See if you can figure out what may have caused this, or if there was anything leading up to it. They found that thing out there, and then all this starts to happen... I don't believe in coincidence. Let's try and find out what the hell it was they really found."

Again, Talmadge tensed, but this time it wasn't anger that rippled through him, it was the satisfaction of opportunity.

"We have to pass security to get to medical," Vuong said, looking at the facility schematics on his holowrist.

"All right. Let's get to Security, then you two, get to medical."

"The information you want would be in the director's files."

Baker turned to Talmadge, who had pulled himself from the wall and was staring at him with a malevolent gaze that buzzed with the controlled thrill of a serial killer outsmarting a detective in an interview.

"Everything they found out there, all the files, everything. That's what I've been trying to get to. You want that information, then there's only one place it will be, and for you to get it, I have to get to the director's office." Sergeant Williams took a deep breath. He'd never played the game before, only heard about it from others, but at that moment, a single word popped into his mind. *Check*. He maintained his composure.

There was no way he was going to allow him to take that anger from him. He needed it to keep moving, to keep clear. "First security, then we'll get you to your precious office." He turned to the others. "Let's go see what happened here."

8

Moisture clung to the air, thick and oppressive, as the environmental system sputtered to life. The hallways felt close and suffocating, the new haze of atmosphere swirling with the ghosts of what had come before. Every shadow seemed to stretch and writhe, reaching for the unit as they crept forward, the darkness alive with silent, desperate hunger.

As they neared the door to security, Dom halted abruptly, his hand rising—a silent command that froze the others in place. For a heartbeat, the world narrowed to the faintest sound: a whisper, so distant and thin it might have been imagined, yet it crawled along his nerves like ice. Inside his helmet, his ears strained, twitching at the edge of panic, as his eyes swept the doorway, searching for movement.

His gaze dropped, and his breath caught. From beneath the sealed door, a thin, viscous stream of blood was oozing out, dark and sluggish, tinged with the watery sheen of melting ice. It crept forward, inch by inch, as if something behind the door was bleeding out into the corridor— something that had only just begun to thaw. The blood slithered past his boots, and for a moment, Dom could almost feel the cold, sticky touch through the suit.

He stared, transfixed, every instinct screaming that something monstrous and unseen was waiting just beyond the threshold— something black and coarse, with claws and fangs, eager for the first sign of life. The others watched the blood snake toward them, the silence so thick it pressed against their chests, and Dom's skin prickled with the certainty that whatever horror had filled these halls was not yet done with them.

Baker signaled Mills and Dom to stack up on opposite sides of the door. He motioned silently for the rest to stay against the wall and then nodded to Dom who reached out and engaged the door switch. The entire unit held their breath, each of them seeing a different horror hiding beyond.

With a hiss the door slid back and something moved within. Baker leveled his rifle, watching as a small object slowly rolled out and started down the incline between them. In the same moment, he realized what it was, and where the blood had come from.

Just inside the door, a small, decapitated body lay sprawled in a grotesque heap. Baker's breath caught as the boy's severed head rolled down the incline, bouncing with a sickening, wet thud each time it struck the uneven floor. The flesh-covered skull spun to a halt at the end of the short hallway, coming to rest with a soft, hollow knock against the leg of a desk that marked the threshold to administration. For a heartbeat, the only movement was the slow, unnatural rotation of the head, its blank, milky eyes staring back at the intruders.

A cold, paralyzing realization slithered through the group, tightening around their chests. Every gaze was locked on the boy's face—dull gray skin, lips parted in a silent scream, one eye rolled back to white, the other fixed in a lifeless stare. The silence was absolute, suffocating; for a moment, it seemed as if the entire station was holding its breath, waiting for something else to move.

Dom tore his eyes away, bile rising in his throat, and forced his trembling hands to bring his weapon up, sweeping the corridor beyond. "Clear," he managed, his voice barely more than a rasp as he swallowed hard, fighting the urge to retch. Whatever nightmare he'd imagined lurking behind the door was nothing compared to the reality before them. The corridor was empty, save for a single light flickering at the far end—its weak glow barely enough to push back the darkness that now felt alive, hungry, and watching.

He hadn't been ready for this. None of them had. And as the echo of the head's final roll faded, every man in the unit knew it would be a long time before their hands stopped shaking.

The unit moved forward, the rest of them averting their gazes as they stepped around the small corpse on the floor. Part of them held their distance as they passed out of respect, but mostly for fear. The feeling one of the tiny, dead arms would reach out to grasp their ankles forced them to give a wide berth.

Baker watched as his men stepped carefully around the body. He knew this was something he was never going to forget, something that would haunt him for as long as breath moved through his lungs. It would be there when he lay down for bed, or passed out on one of the benders he guaranteed himself he was going to have once he got back. He also knew that some of his unit would never be the same. He knew well what seeing things like this could do to a person, the things that happen to a man mentally when they realize the full capacity for human violence and depravity. He could already see it creeping through their eyes. Rwanda had been bad, but this was something entirely different all together. For some of them, this would be their last trip out. Transfers to different units would be coming, that he knew, and where he would normally feel betrayed, hurt by their leaving, this time he couldn't blame them. They'd be stupid not to.

The group went a short ways ahead before they saw the sign that read security. Just outside the door was another body, a security officer still in uniform. The man's sidearm lay a few feet away and Baker could see instantly that the gun's slide had jammed. Across the hall was another, this one lying on its back with six gunshots perforating its chest. The man against the wall sat sprawled out, his head hanging at a strange angle, loose and off centered. As he neared, he could see that the guard's neck had been snapped, the force of it nearly wrenching the head free from the shoulders.

As they drew closer, Fascio reached down and pulled a pack of cigarettes that were sticking out of the guard's vest pocket free. He looked at the man's face for a moment before reaching down and shutting the eyes.

Then he rose to his feet.

"I thought you quit," Vuong said as Fascio turned the pack over in his hands.

Fascio turned his head. His gaze blank beneath pale skin, an ivory contrasted to the usual pink and red it held. He stared at Vuong for a moment before sliding the pack into the pocket of his envirosuit and turning to make his way next to the room.

"That hallway there," Vuong said, pointing a little ways down the corridor they were in. "It'll lead you through central housing. Follow the hallway until it curves to the right, and medical will be the first door on your left. There should be signs. I'm sure you won't miss it."

"Let me know the moment you find something out," Baker added.

"Rah," Dom replied flatly, nodding to Lanskey, who turned to follow him.

Baker watched the pair depart, a tingling creeping up his spine, radiating outwards like a pair of rotted wings crawling across his back as he told himself that the two would be fine. He took a deep breath, watching as they disappeared out of view further down the hall. Another mistake.

"All right, Vuong, let's see what we can find."

As the men entered, the first thing they noticed was the bullet holes that riddled the curved hallway leading to the small reception area. Wilkes took point, his rifle at the ready. He realized immediately that it had been a one-sided firefight. The wall near the entrance was pockmarked beyond recognition, but the rest of the room was clean. Whoever had been firing was trying to keep someone or something out. He made his way further in and stopped just inside. On his right was a small security post, spider webbed polyacrylic glass, cubing in a small security console. The inside was empty, but he quickly noticed the door had been yanked clear of the jam; splinters of wood and twisted metal sticking outwards where the handle touched the wall. "Clear," he called out as the others cautiously made their way in. It had taken an immense amount of force to yank it clear, and for a brief second, he found himself grateful that he had not been there when it happened.

Behind them the station had begun to come back to life. Metal creaked and groaned as the cold dissipated and the entire structure expanded. There were loud cracks snapping around them and down the long corridors. It sounded as though the entire facility was slowly being wrenched apart.

"We need something to get through that door," Talmadge said, noticing that the door to the security room was still sealed, and deciding to make himself useful. If he wanted to get what he needed, he at least had to lower their hatred of him, or at least do something to help them forget it temporarily.

"I have a better idea," Baker said, turning to glance at Wilkes. "Torch'll cut through that right?"

Wilkes nodded, pulling out the small device and stepping to the tiny booth. He fired up the torch and slowly cut his way through the shatterproof glass. The material popped and hissed as small beads of molten glass dripped to the floor below. A thin stream of acrid smoke rose up to hover across the ceiling for a moment before being wisped away into the ventilation duct. When he'd cut a circle big enough for his arm to fit, he reached through and engaged the switch that unlocked the reinforced door to the security room. Behind him, Baker waited, his gaze locked to the steel door blocking their way. Inwardly, a small part of him hoped the door wouldn't open. As the room crackled with bluish-white light he realized he didn't have much desire to find out what had truly happened. It was his job, and by protocol he needed to find out, but deep down, he begged for an excuse to just go back to the ship, lift off and file a report back home.

"This is the trip," he whispered silently to himself.
The door popped free, the small light on the handle turning green.

Baker signaled Fascio who moved forward to open the door. He gently pushed it inwards, his pistol drawn before stepping in. The back wall to the room was lined with dozens of monitors. In front of them was a single chair, a body slouched over in it. On the floor next to the chair was a pistol, and he could see by the splatter hanging from the ceiling what had happened without even looking.

"Get that cleared up," Baker snapped, turning to Vuong. "I want eyes on this facility, like yesterday."

"Roger that, Sarge," he replied, waiting for Mills and Fascio to finish rolling the chair with the corpse in it out of the room.

*What in the hell happened here...?* Baker pondered again.

As soon as the body was out of the way, Vuong moved to the console, hitting a series of switches which brought it to life.

A few minutes later, Vuong turned to Sarge. "I can get in, but it's gonna take some time to figure out where everything is. This system's a mess. Whoever used it last, encrypted half the files, and the system's completely out of whack. I need to realign surveillance, patch back into the optical network and access the drive files before I can even start looking. That's gonna take me some time."

Baker nodded, moving aside as Fascio returned the chair to the console, a thin fabric covering the burgundy stain beneath.

"Roger that. You stay here and work on getting that sorted out. The rest of you are on me. And Vuong, you let me know the moment you find anything useful."

"Will do," Vuong replied as the others turned to make their way out. "And, Sarge."

"What is it, Corporal?"

"Feel free to lock the door on your way out."

Baker nodded, turning to follow the others back into the hallway.

As the door closed behind them, Vuong pulled his pistol and set it on the console in front of him. Almost instantly, the walls began to press in on him, and the hidden eyes in the dark corners began to stare. "Alright then. Let's see what we got."

9

The unit made their way down and across the corridor to the hallway leading to central housing. As they neared, Fascio crackled across the comms. "You know, I've had this really fucked up feeling since the moment we arrived. I don't exactly know how to explain it, but it feels like something's watching us, waiting to jump out and tear us apart. Like this whole station's just been waiting for us to let down our guard."

"Well, you can keep that shit to yourself, Fascio. None of us need to be hearing that right now. I don't do supernatural, so you can just pack that right away."

"Just saying, Sarge."

"Yeah," Wilkes added. "It's like the place is analyzing us; the shadows, the darkness, everything."

"That's exactly what I'm saying," Fascio replied quickly. "Something's not right here."

"No shit, Marine," Baker replied, glancing at a man lying face down with a knife handle sticking out of his back. "I didn't notice that. Thank you for enlightening me of our current situation."

"I think it has something to do with whatever it was they found out there."

"And again, Corporal, you aren't paid to think, so keep that shit to yourself."

"Just saying."

"Well don't."

"This is housing," Talmadge clicked in as the group passed the first of the units. "We have space for forty-five families to live comfortably—"

"Don't start with that shit again, Talmadge!" Baker barked, cutting him off mid-breath. "So far, all we've seen are bodies, so there aren't no fucking families up here. There's no smiles, no laughter, no happy bouncing babies. What you have is a station full of dead colonists. That's what you have."

"Sarge..."

Baker stopped, turning to look at Fascio, who stood staring into one of the housing units just ahead.

"Look."

The sergeant stepped forward, peering into the doorway that led to one of the housing units. There was a dim light flickering from deeper inside, shadows dancing across the inner hall from a room beyond.

"Pie it," Baker said, glancing in both directions before looking back to the marine who slung his rifle and had already leveled his pistol.

Fascio made his way in, Mills entering close behind. He crept delicately down the hall, ignoring the pictures that hung; portraits of a young couple standing happy against the red planet's backdrop. He made his way to the first door and slowly opened it, his pistol taking the lead. Inside was a small bedroom, a handful of toys scattered along the floor and a tiny bed draped in a cartoon character blanket. He felt his chest tighten ever so slightly as he gave it a quick sweep and moved further in. Seeing dead adults didn't sit well with him, but the children... Children held a special place of sadness in his chest. As he got closer to the illuminated doorway he entered into what was a small dining area. There was a wooden table set with three chairs around it and a final meal laid out across it. The trays of food sat untouched, moist, covered in rot and melting mold. Food had been served and he could see that a family had just sat down for a meal, but never got the chance to consume it. He turned to continue further in when a small stain on the floor caught his eye, followed by another. Leading further into the unit was a small trail of blood that built with each step as he went deeper within, the droplets growing to splatter and the splatter growing to pools. He approached the flashing doorway and peered cautiously around, Wilkes standing ready just behind him. Inside he was greeted by an empty bedroom, the flashing light coming from a small holographic picture sitting atop a bedside table. He approached slowly, the flickering of the light disorienting his vision for the blink of a moment. Then he saw the trail continue into a small room off to the side. As he stepped towards it, Mills glanced at the flashing picture. Now there was another addition to the family, a young boy. Fascio walked towards the small room and stopped when he reached the door. He could feel his stomach drop as he peered in, his pulse beginning to pound heavily in his ears.

Just inside was a small bathroom.

Propped against the company-issue bathtub was the corpse of a younger man, his body twisted in a final, agonized spasm. In one hand, he still clutched a straight razor, its blade slick and red. At a glance, Fascio could see the deep, ragged gashes slashed into both wrists—wounds so severe they had severed flesh and bone, leaving the arms grotesquely mangled.

Face-up in the tub lay the body of a young boy, his skin waxen and blue, dark purple lines circling his tiny throat. He was entombed in a pool of slowly melting ice, the water tinged with blood and the cold unable to hide the violence that had taken place.

Fascio felt his breath catch, his legs threatening to buckle beneath him. The room spun, vertigo clawing at his senses as he struggled to process the horror before him. He had seen his share of atrocities—war had shown him the worst humanity could offer—but nothing had prepared him for this. The sight of a father and son, destroyed by a violence so intimate and final, pierced deeper than any battlefield memory.

How could anyone do something like that to their own child? The question echoed in his mind, unanswered and unbearable, as the cold dread settled into his bones.

He turned slowly, putting his hand on Wilkes' chest and shook his head to the side. There was no need for both of them to have to carry what he now would. No need for anyone else to ever see that. So, as he stepped out of the room he pulled the door closed behind him and followed Wilkes out, leaving the visceral pain to ebb within the confines of the sealed unit.

"Anything?" Baker asked as the pair exited the unit.

Fascio shook his head, allowing his eyes to tell Sarge everything. There was nothing alive.

"Alright. Let's keep moving."

They continued on, passing more derelict apartments, all gazes falling to a door that was broken inwards, splintered and cracked, with a man lying face down just inside, a fire axe buried deep in his back. The weight around them pressed in even heavier.

The facility had begun to come more and more alive around them; a loose cable hanging from the ceiling ahead sparking as electricity now flowed back through the complex. Metal groaned as the atmosphere continued to bend and stretch the steel framing, and blood, frozen in place prior, had begun to liquefy and congeal. Outside their envirosuits, the metallic smell of death began to waft into the air, rising upwards like a cloud of sulfur as the facility began to rot around them, festering as the reintroduction of oxygen allowed life to continue its natural course of decay.

"That leads to medical," Talmadge said as they exited housing into the main corridor that snaked through the complex. He started to tell them how their medical facility had state-of-the art-equipment, some of which wasn't even available on Earth yet, but closed his mouth as the words began to form. He took a deep breath, staring at the sergeant's back as they started towards the med wing. He forced himself to keep it cool. He'd already drafted every report and statement in his head and even sat through the imaginary hearing that would strip the man of his rank under dereliction of duty and a number of other violations. He had seen the faces of the council as they read him his sentence, faces he knew well, smiles he had shared many company fundraisers with. Inwardly he grinned, a ripple of excitement flashing through him. The sergeant thought he was in command, but so had many others before him, others that had built the steps he had used to climb higher.

Steam vented downwards from the ceiling as they walked through the doorway leading to the medical wing. It fell like a clouded mist, trailing down the wall and dissipating just before hitting the floor where it was quickly sucked in by an intake duct at the base. Overhead, lights flickered lightly, the darkness of the facility phasing in and out, a pulsing heartbeat that struggled to hold the crushing shadows at bay.

As they entered into the main hall, their eyes fell to a neatly organized row of black plastic bags, each sticking out of the wall on both sides, lined from one end to the other, some stacked two high further down.

"How many died before all this went down?" Wilkes asked as he subconsciously counted the body bags they passed.

Baker ignored the question, his eyes scanning the light grey surface of the hallway ahead. He could see a command module with a lightly lit panel behind it; a nurse's station abandoned by everything but a leaning stack of file folders and medical supplies. There were a series of lights along the console that flickered orange and red in the dark, casting a flame-like illumination overhead.

As they made their way further they could see signs of a firefight that had occurred; bullet holes pockmarking the walls and a pile of bodies at the end of a short hall they passed; all wearing medical lab coats, a ruffled pile of red stained white. As they passed the nurse's station, Baker held up his hand. His eyes scanned both hallways that led off in different directions. The signs overhead read *Surgery-Observation-Morgue*, and the one leading the opposite direction; *Nursing-Administration-Pediatrics*.

He felt a shudder run through him as his eyes fell to the first sign. He exhaled softly, a silent scoff stifled within. *This entire station's a morgue...*

"The medical director's office is in administration," Talmadge said after a moment, his voice startling the others who stood silently behind.

"Then we go that way," Baker said, glancing one last time at the other sign, a small relief washing through him that they didn't have to see what was down that hall.

He turned and started towards admin, glancing quickly at the stack of files on the desk and the dozens of names sticking out in colored tape from the flaps. All those names were now dead. Everything was dead, except for them.

A short way down the corridor, the lighting disappeared, replaced with small overhead emergency lights that glowed faintly against the pressing black. Atmosphere wafted upwards from the floor vents, the anti-slip material beneath disappearing in some spots alltogether. The light grey became splotched, with splatter trailing down the walls to more body bags taking up space on the floor, these much less organized than those at the entrance. Ahead of them a single gurney lay toppled on its side, a still corpse lying next to it with an IV unit still attached at the arm. As they passed, dead eyes stared up at them from a bloated face, gray splotched with purple and brown.

The makeshift triage spread from one end of the hall to the other— a patchwork of blood and gore littered with body bags and corpses. Above, a ventilation pipe hung down, hissing angrily as it spit condensation at their feet as they passed.

Wilkes stepped past, his arms trembling as he realized that his hands had cramped from squeezing the grip on his rifle. He could feel the flesh beneath his suit, covered in a layer of sweat, hot and clammy. There was a crippling uneasiness clawing at him and he fought desperately against the urge to turn around and run as fast as he could back to the ship. The station dug into him; peeled at his suit, and every corpse he walked past was waiting to spring to life and tear him from his suit to devour him. He could feel his heart pounding in his chest, blood beating heavily against his eardrums, and he knew that he was going to burst at any moment. Then, Sarge's voice snapped across the comms and pulled him back to the dimly lit hallway he was in, the panic slowly releasing its grip around his throat.

"Administration is on the left. Let's see if Lanskey has found anything out. Then we'll get Mr. impatient here to the director's office. After that, I think it's safe to say, we can get the hell off this rock. I don't wanna be here one second more than I have to, and it doesn't look like there's anything left for us to see."

Wilkes exhaled deeply at Sarge's words. *Thank you…*

Twenty feet later they were making their way into the administration's section. A series of office style doors lined the short hallway, with a single door at the end that read, *Director Thomas,* on a small plaque above.

They made their way to the door and paused, exchanging glances before Fascio reached out and pressed the door switch. With a hiss it slid to the side and the small room opened up before them.

Lanskey turned quickly in her chair, Dom spinning at the sound of the door activating, his finger jerking against the trigger instinctively before he heard the intruder shout across his comm.

Fascio jerked to the side, shouting, "Jesus Christ, Dom! It's us," as the other jerked his arm at the last second, sending a stray round blasting against the wall next to the door. "Fuck!"

"God damnit, Fascio," Dom yelled, lowering his rifle as he stepped towards the door. "Fucking tell me when you're gonna sneak up on us like that. I almost dropped you just now."

"What in the *hell* are you thinking Marine?" Baker stepped into the room with anger blazing in his gaze. "You pull that shit again and I swear to God I'll shoot you myself." He paused, turning to the other directly behind him. "Wilkes, would you kindly relieve DiLeonardo of his firearm."

"Sarge?" Dom said, starting to object, but instantly ceasing his plea as he saw the anger burning behind his sergeant's eyes. He'd messed up, and regardless of his fear, or the state or their mission and the facility around them, he had shot at one of his fellow soldiers... He held out his rifle as Wilkes stepped over to him.

"Sorry, man," Wilkes mouthed as he took Dom's rifle and stepped back to the sergeant.

"You wait your ass in that hallway," Baker growled. He didn't even want Dom in the same room at the moment, and wrestled heavy against the urge to punch him in the side of the face as he walked past. If he had lost a man at the hands of one of his own... *Fucking idiot...* He pushed the thought back and turned his attention back to Lanskey, taking a deep breath and waiting for the footsteps to disappear behind him before speaking.

"What do you got for us, Doc?"

"I didn't find anything at first, Sarge, just the usual reports of space-sickness associated with atmospheric conditioning, and the common cold. Normal things that occur with the adjustment to deep space living. But then things began to get interesting. Right around the time they began unearthing whatever it is that they found, reports started coming in of patients experiencing severe headaches, disorientation and hallucinations. I have cases here of patients hearing voices, seeing relatives and friends they say had died years prior." She paused, staring at Baker for a moment before continuing. "There is one thing that they all seem to have in common though. Every person reported hearing some type of whispering. Like a faint voice they couldn't quite understand. I don't think this is related to faulty atmospheric processing or artificial environment, and I ruled out classic isolation sickness; or cabin fever by simple terms." She turned back to the console and pulled up a string of reports; dozens of names scrolling down the page. "A short time after these reports began coming in, the instances of physical injuries and suicide began to rise. Then, a week after, they skyrocketed. The doctors on the facility began treating more patients than they could handle. It looks like they were almost out of supplies even before the main outbreak occurred."

"My question, is why was none of this reported?" Baker asked, his gaze moving to the names still scrolling downwards. "Why did none of this get out? Nobody thought to tell the company what was going on?"

"My only thought was that someone sabotaged the communications array before anyone had a chance to."

"But why the hell would someone do that?" Baker paused, taking a deep breath as he stared at the console. "None of this makes sense."

"That's not all, Sergeant. I found something else."
Baker lifted his gaze.
"All the patients reported seeing something in the facility, a shimmer of some sort, or ripple in the atmosphere. There are dozens of reports, all describing the same thing in different ways, but the same thing nonetheless. Maybe something went wrong with environmental, maybe the atmosphere mixture was tampered with, I don't know, but shortly after that, the reports stopped."

"People stopped seeing whatever it was they were seeing?"

Silence worked between them as Lanskey stared into his eyes.

"No. There were no more doctors to file them."

Baker took everything in, his gaze moving to the screen in front of him as the names scrolling downwards stopped, a curser blinking at the bottom of the last name. Wierzbowski. "Talmadge," he said after a moment, his eyes still locked to the screen. "You know more about this station than any of us. Would it be possible for something like that to happen? Could someone have tampered with atmosphere controls or environment, other than

obviously shutting it off?"

"No," Talmadge replied quietly from the doorway. "The canisters used to create the atmosphere are premixed on Earth, and the converters that are designed to kick in after they run out, simply convert the planet's atmosphere into a breathable atmosphere in the station. There's no way for anyone to alter that. There's not even a backdoor in programming. It was sealed before the station went online."

"Doc?"

"I have to side with Talmadge on this one. Even if someone could have tampered with the environmental systems in here, there has never been anything recorded that would lead me to believe what has occurred here, was environment or atmosphere related. This had to be something else."

"Sarge..."

Vuong's voice cracked through the comms unit, pulling his attention away from the screen in front.

"I read you, what have you got for me?"

"You should get back to security. There's something I think you need to see."

"What is it, Vuong?" Baker asked, the tone behind the other's voice raising the hairs at the base of his scalp.

"I've accessed the station-wide surveillance archives."

There was a pause. A deep silence hung in the air as Baker waited for him to continue.

"Just... I don't think I can describe it. You should really get back here."

The knot twisting in his gut wrenched tighter as the skin across his back pulled taught. "Hold tight. We're on our way."

Baker looked to Lanskey who was still watching him over her shoulder, one hand poised on the keyboard. "You mentioned you had no belief this thing was airborne right? You don't believe this is something communicable?"

Lanskey shook her head. "No, Sir. There's no recorded traces of toxins, or any airborne anomalies on any of the sensors. Whatever's caused this, it's something else."

"Okay. Good. Then it's safe to assume we no longer need the suits?"

"Atmosphere is one hundred percent, and environment has already begun leveling out. It's still gonna be a little chilly for a while, but yes, I'd say we're about as safe as we're going to be in here."

Baker clicked to an open channel. "All right everyone, you heard the lady. Let's stow these suits. We may need what's left in the tanks later. Corlin, Hawkes, what's your status?"

"En route Sarge," Corlin replied behind a layer of static. "Passing comms now."

"Copy that, Corporal, meet us in security, Vuong has something for us."

"Roger that."

Baker hit the button on the envirosuit's belt pack.

There was a small click as the thin, nano-based fabric unsealed at his back and it was pulled inside the small rectangular box at his waist. He inhaled heavily, taking a deep breath of stale metallic tinged air and exhaling it in front of him. He was glad to be out of the suit. He'd always felt claustrophobic in it, and no matter how many times he'd put it on, he couldn't wait to hit that button. He wiped his hands on his fatigues and removed his helmet long enough to wipe the sweat from his brow and run his hand across his shaved head. Then he fastened his helmet back into place and turned to the others.

"Let's go see what Vuong has found for us." He turned to Wilkes. "Corporal, you stay with Dom and Lanskey. I'll click you when we find out what Vuong has. Keep me posted on what you find here. I wanna know the second anything new comes up, you got that?" His nose wrinkled as the distant odor of death began to waft past.

"Aye-firm."

"And give DiLeonardo his weapon back. But reteach him where the fucking safety is."

Dom looked at the sergeant, embarrassment flushing his face as he watched them walk away.

"Good one, Dom," Wilkes said as he walked up and held out the rifle. "Perfect timing as always..."

10

Time crept by, the seconds morphing to minutes, the latter making space for larger increments that passed imperceptibly. The smell of the facility had already begun to permeate the air, piercing the intruder's nostrils as it filtered past in rancid wafts. They made their way back towards security, the sensation of endless backtracking and retracing of their steps beginning to wear on them. As they passed housing, Fascio stopped long enough to close the doors to the units they had passed. As he closed the last door, he paused, his gaze falling to the floor for a moment. He was still struggling to shake the image of the little boy half exposed in a sheet of ice from his head. He knew the tub would have been mostly melted by now, and lamented the fact that he could see the boy floating in a still pool of water, bloated and purple, skin loose and translucent, with his dead father next to him. He realized that by now the boy's dead eyes would be staring at the ceiling through the stagnant water, yellowed and dull, and he cursed his mind for not being able to resist conjuring the sickening image. He felt moisture tugging at the corner of his eyes and his mouth beginning to salivate as bile crept upwards from his stomach. Apathetic to his pain, the facility continued to groan around him as its cold steel and titanium skeleton flexed.

"Are you good, Fascio?"

He startled. "Uh… Yeah, Sarge, sorry."

"Just hold it together, Marine," Baker said as he walked past, placing his hand on his shoulder for a moment. "We'll all be out of here soon, then it's mai tais and piña coladas on a Mexican beach."

Fascio nodded softly, turning to follow Talmadge and the sergeant as they made their way into the main corridor.

"What do you got for me?" Baker asked as he stepped into the room.

"This place sounds like it's falling apart," Vuong said, turning to look at Sarge, who stood impatiently waiting for the report.

Baker stared at him. He thought it would have been more accurate to say that it sounded like the station was being ripped apart, but he wasn't here to discuss semantics.

"Okay." Vuong spun his chair and clicked across the keyboard, pulling up a still image of a woman sitting at a desk in what appeared to be one of the unit's bedrooms. "It took some digging, but I managed to access the personnel logs. I thought, if we wanted to learn what happened here, what better source than the people it happened to as it was happening." He glanced over his shoulder for a moment, exhaling loudly, bringing the video to life.

"I can't begin to describe how amazing this is," the woman began, her eyes full of excitement and life. Baker's focus fell to the slender woman with neatly brushed hair smiling back. If it wasn't for the death

97

that surrounded them, and the fact that this woman was undoubtedly just another corpse releasing noxious fumes into the air, he would have almost found her pretty. "Never would I have imagined that our family would be among the first humans to colonize Mars. I was so surprised when Paul agreed, you know, with Brandon being so young still. But I think he realized that the situation on Earth wasn't going to get any better. Maybe he thought we'd have a better opportunity out here. Either way, I'm just happy he said yes. It's surreal; I mean, just looking out the window is like… It's unbelievable." She sighed heavily, the smile growing slightly. "They're still working on getting the basic social structures in place; the school and community center, but for the most part, we've all settled in to our daily routine. I work in the labs, and Paul is on the survey team. They've set up a basic daycare system for the parents. Brandon doesn't seem to mind. He says he misses his friends, but I think he's getting acclimated to the new change." Behind the desk a little boy stepped into the room. "Mom, can I play my holo-game?" The woman turned and nodded. "Yes, just turn it off when your father gets home." She turned back to the camera, sighing with the lingering smile before reaching her hand out to click the video off, pausing at the last second. "I'm really happy, Mom, and I know you didn't want me to leave, but this is the best thing we could have done. I hope you understand."

Fascio stared at the screen, the face of the little boy stabbing him in the chest. He turned his gaze to the floor to avoid the others. There was a vice around his heart and it was wrenching tighter. The boy in the video was wearing the same light blue shirt and bright green shorts...

As Vuong was about to explain that there was more, Corlin and Hawkes entered the room.

"Message was sent, Sarge," Corlin said as the others nodded to their return. "Guess there was some issue with Portofino's headset, minor malfunction. I switched it out. Should be working fine now."

"Portofino, do you read me?"

"I read you, Sarge. Loud and clear."

"I want comms check every hour at the top, starting now. I will not have us stranded on this rock because you've got a faulty wire, you understand?"

"Copy that, Sergeant."

"Good. What's the status of my ship?"

"We're green across the board, ready to go when you are, Sir."

"Good. Keep her that way, over and out."

He turned his focus back to Vuong and nodded.

The private took a deep breath and exhaled slowly. "Here's another one. This one's dated a week later." He pressed play and edged back from the screen, rubbing the sweat that had begun to build across his palms on his pants.

The monitor came to life again, with the same woman sitting at the desk. Baker could see that something was off. The woman had dark rings under her eyes and her hair was messy and unkempt. There was a slight redness to her eyes and it looked like a long lack of sleep mixed with tears. She stared at the screen without blinking for a moment before her voice cracked through the small speakers. "I haven't been sleeping well. None of us have. I keep hearing, voices. Like a whisper, hidden in the shadows. Nobody's talking about it, but I know everyone else is hearing it too. Nobody wants to admit it for fear of landing a psych evaluation. I asked Paul. He said I was imagining it, and there was nothing to worry about. But I came home from work yesterday and he was staring into the closet. He didn't see me... He was talking to someone." The woman looked down at her lap for a moment. "I don't know what's happening, but people are dying. We had three accidents at the lab yesterday, and there were four in processing. Maybe people are... I think we're all just tired." The woman looked back up at the screen, her puffy eyes filled with concern. "The survey team found something out there. Some type of—*structure*. They think it's alien. What are we doing here?" The woman stared at the monitor for another minute before letting her gaze fall to her lap again. Then her gaze lifted to the camera. "I know it sounds crazy, but I saw my uncle Phillip yesterday.

He was standing outside our window. My uncle's been dead for ten years... He wanted something.

I'm not sure." Her gaze turned to the wall. Then she reached out and turned the recording off.

Baker stared at the blank monitor before letting his gaze fall to the back of Vuong's head. Dread began to worm in, eating at his skin just beneath the first layer. Even though temperature regulation was online, he felt his skin begin to prickle.

"There's more," Vuong said softly, clicking on the next video. "This is four days later."

On the monitor was the same woman. She looked nervous and was beginning to stammer when something spooked her from behind and she turned, her chair landing noisily on the floor before bolting out of the room and disappearing into the hallway. The video continued recording the empty room behind.

"I skipped ahead a bit," Vuong said, moving the timeline on the video ahead. When it started again, the timestamp showed that two hours had passed. Baker squinted at the screen, moving slightly closer to Vuong's chair. On the monitor, a shadow moved in the hallway; moments later being replaced with the little boy from the earlier video. The boy stood in the doorway, staring at the camera blankly, his face dirty, with dark stains splashed across the front of his clothing; the same from the first video. There were lines down his face where tears had run through the dirt.

Behind him, a banging sound echoed through the hall. They could hear a man yelling for him to unlock the door, that he just wanted to protect him. The boy turned and darted down the hall. A minute later the banging stopped with a loud crack, the sound of the front door breaking away from the latch that held it tight. Seconds later the man walked past the room without glancing, heading in the direction the little boy had run.

Fascio felt his skin tighten as his legs began to tremble.

"It gets worse, Sarge..."
Fascio turned his gaze from the screen.
Vuong clicked another video. This time the camera showed the interior of the main airlock. The door opened up as a man in an envirosuit stepped in. He looked disoriented, his gaze locked to the floor. Baker felt a shiver run up his arms. After a moment, the man reached to the pack at his belt and disengaged the suit. Baker watched as he stood there for a moment, staring blankly at the floor before lifting his gaze to the outer airlock door. There was no sound, but he could see his lips moving, words being directed at the empty space before him for a moment before he stepped forward and engaged the outer seal. In an instant all the air was sucked from the room and the man brought his hands to his throat, gasping for air before falling to his knees and then crumpling to his side. Baker

stood there, watching as blood began to pour from the man's eyes and ears before Vuong reached up and turned the video off.

The security room stayed silent, the only sound coming from a distant creak of metal. The men were struggling to register what they had just seen. Walking past it in the halls, their imagination allowed them to create all manner of rational explanations, but witnessing it in person. There was nothing rational, nothing sane. Each of them wrestled with the horror that sat frozen on the monitor.

"There are dozens of these," Vuong said, slowly turning in his chair. "Every person in this facility either killed themselves, or took as many people as possible with them before they did. I've checked every camera, every angle and watched the last fifty video logs. Everyone in

this station's dead, Sarge. Every one of them."

"What in the hell did they find out there?" Sarge whispered, his gaze moving to the still image of the dead man in the airlock frozen on the screen.

"I," Talmadge started, pausing to correct himself.

"We need to get to the director's office."

Baker stayed quiet. The weight of what he had just seen sat heavy in his chest. He had no doubt in his mind, whatever it was that had caused all this; whatever had killed this entire facility, or caused the people living there to kill themselves and everyone else in it, came from whatever it was they found out there. He needed to find out what that was, and make sure whatever it was, wasn't now hunting them as well. He moved his gaze to Vuong who sat quietly looking up at him. "Keep searching. See what else you can find. There's gotta be something that can help us figure out what's going on here. Look for anything out of the ordinary."

"Sarge, none of this is ordinary."
"You know what I mean, Corporal. Just keep looking."

Vuong nodded, turning back to the monitor.

"I'm gonna stay here with Vuong and review the files. The rest of you are going to get Talmadge here to the director's office. Let's find out what the hell it is that they found out there."

11

The stench of decay was relentless, thickening with every step, festering in the stagnant air. Even with the environmental regulators humming and the filtration systems working overtime, the odor of rot seemed to ooze from the very walls of Attis, as if the station itself was decomposing from within. The sour reek of congealed blood clung to their suits, heavy and metallic, a coppery-iron film that coated their tongues and burned in their nostrils. It was a smell that didn't just linger—it invaded, worming its way into their memories, promising to haunt them long after they left.

Fascio's thoughts flickered to the medical wing, to Lanskey, Dom, and Wilkes, and he shuddered at the thought of what they must be enduring. If the stench here was this bad, what horrors awaited in the heart of the slaughter?

They turned into the corridor for administration, and the horror only deepened. The main reception area loomed ahead, a large desk and two monitors sitting like silent sentinels. The tan plasticrete walls were plastered with Xenocorp posters—smiling workers, pristine uniforms, a child with a perfect smudge of oil on her cheek. The images, bright and hopeful, were a grotesque parody against the backdrop of darkness and death. The posters' glossy surfaces reflected the emergency lights in warped, mocking smiles, their promises of "Better Planets for All" twisted by the reality of the carnage.

The contrast was almost nauseating. The only section of the facility with thin, soft carpet underfoot, meant to comfort visitors, now muffled the footsteps of the living as they walked among the dead. The carpet, once beige, was stained in places with dark, spreading patches—reminders that no amount of corporate polish could cover up the rot beneath.

Everywhere, the sense of something wrong pressed in. The air felt heavier here, as if the station itself was holding its breath, waiting for the next horror to reveal itself. The silence was not empty, but watchful, and every step forward felt like an intrusion into a tomb that did not want to be disturbed.

They made their way past, following the sign that led to accounting and officers. By the time the facility would have been finished, it would have become a multi-trillion dollar investment, housing thousands of families; a self-sustaining city spanning dozens of miles. And this was the first of hundreds they had already blueprinted out. If things had gone as planned, they would have had atmospheric processors up and running and advanced terraforming in production within the decade. That projection looked like it had just gotten a bit longer in the tooth.

"It should be the last office at the end," Talmadge said, Fascio picking up the slight spring that had entered his step. The rep had finally managed to get his way. It was a physical struggle for him to stifle his excitement, the burning necessity to stifle any information leaks ignited like coals beneath him. He needed to contain the situation and make sure any incriminating evidence was locked behind so many doors that by the time anyone managed to get clearance to search, the incident would be a long forgotten hiccup in a long series of successful planet transformations. He pushed back a smile and continued further.

They continued down the quiet corridor when the lights above flickered for a moment before going black.

"What the fuck..," Hawkes whispered, the soft shuffle of rifles shifting to the ready around him as the emergency lights along the walls came to life.

The group clicked on their flashlights and kept their weapons at the ready, their pace slower, more cautious as the station continued to taunt them. Shadows glistened against the light, the sheen of condensation casting flickering reflections off the smooth surfaces. Fascio could feel unseen eyes peering into him as he moved quietly forward, his feet squishing against the moist carpet underfoot.

"Stay sharp," Mills said, his voice just barely above a whisper. "Let's not have any surprises." His eyes scanned the corridor ahead. Then he keyed up his holowrist, which was now synced to the station. "Systems normal. Reads like a power surge."

"Man," Fascio grumbled. "I'd give my left nut for a set of night vision right now."

"Yeah," Mills whispered back. "Well, we don't have any, so suck it up."

Fascio and Hawkes shifted nervously, Mills spinning at the back of the group, his rifle raised at the shadows that followed them as he walked backwards for the next few paces.

The hallway ahead curved slightly and the soldiers slowed as they approached. The darkness around them was heavy, a weight that pressed in on all sides, suffocating blackness deeper than the space they traveled through on their journey there. As they continued on, their eyes began to played tricks, tiny shards of light and shapes in the darkness reaching out with grasping fingers as they passed around the thin beams from their flashlights.

Fascio was the first around and as he entered the bend he paused, holding his fist in the air to signal the others to stop. He flashed his light across a shape in the hallway ahead, the dark stain splashed across the wall behind it telling him immediately what it was. He brought his hand down and started forward, the overhead lights flickering for a moment before holding steady again. As he neared the body that was slumped over against the wall, something caught his eye. In the dead man's hand was an antique shotgun, Earth model; early twenty-first century.

The dull steel was locked in the man's grasp, with the carbon stock leaned across his legs. The blood spray shot up the wall to the ceiling where tiny holes dotted the space above. Fascio paused for a second before kneeling down and wrenching the weapon from the man's grip. He saw a box of cartridges sticking out of the man's jacket pocket and pulled them out, looking them over for a moment before placing them in his vest pouch. As he rose up he could see a look of disgust across Talmadge's face.

"What? Don't think he's gonna be needing it any time soon."

Talmadge scrunched his lips and squinted at him for a moment, silently disapproving of him touching the corpse.

"How much farther, Talmadge?" Mills asked, pulling the deadlocked gaze that had happened apart.

"Just up ahead," he replied, a metallic groan echoing his words deeper in the facility.

"Well, there's no sense standing around."

Fascio pulled his gaze away and moved further down the hall. As he came to another sharp curve the overhead lights flickered back to life, casting their sterile glow back across the walls. He found himself beginning to question whether it was simply a glitch in the electrical system, or if there wasn't something more sinister at work. Again, he forced the feeling back down, Sergeant Thomas' words filling his ears. *Keep that superstitious shit to yourself...* He was right, too. It was doing nothing to help his situation, and the feeling of panic was only thinly held behind his resolve.

They made it another ten feet down the hall when Fascio saw a sign above the last door that read; Director Jeremy Thomas.

"That's it," Talmadge said, stepping towards the door.

"Whoa," Mills snapped, slapping his hand against the rep's chest, stopping his movement. "It don't work like that." He stared at the man for a moment before calling to his companion. "Fascio. Pie it."

Fascio nodded, turning to the side of the doorway before reaching across and opening the door. He pushed it gently, swinging it open, and then swung around with his rifle raised. Inside, the room was empty. The desk at the back of the room was neat and orderly and there was a half-empty bottle of American whiskey on top with a glass next to it. Along one wall was a bookshelf, dozens of spines sticking out, ripples of brown and beige with stripes of color between: manuals for everything in the facility. "Clear."

Back in security Baker and Vuong filtered through video after video. It was the same scene, death and chaos, colonists running, hiding, killing and dying.

"Can you pinpoint when all this shit started?" Baker asked, pulling his gaze from the monitor.

"Pretty sure," Vuong replied. "It's just gonna take a little while. I have to keep going back until things look normal, and then move forward from there."

"Do it," Baker replied, turning around and stepping into the room outside. He opened a channel on his comm. "Lanskey, you have anything for me?"

"Nothing new Sarge," she replied a moment later. "I've poured through medical and toxicology reports from the first victims. Everything is coming back normal. There's no signs of any physiological changes. This has to be something else, but all the other scenarios don't make any sense. The symptoms are... unique."

"All right. Keep looking, and let me know when you find something."

"Copy that."

Talmadge sat behind the director's desk in a plush synthetic leather chair, or possibly authentic leather, though that would have been illegal after the ban of animal based furniture. But again, Xenocorp had ways of making things happen for those that held more prominent positions in the company, and nobody was sending authenticators or animal rights reps to Mars  just to check an administrator's furniture. He pulled file after file from the computer and began putting it onto a nanodrive he had pulled from his jacket pocket. On the other side of the room, Hawkes stood at the doorway, peering down the hallway, watching the shadows that had crept back into the dark spaces. Fascio had pulled one of the manuals from a shelf on the wall and was browsing it, when he slapped it shut and tossed it on the floor. Talmadge looked up from the screen, every sense in him yelling for him to pick the manual up and put it back where it belonged, his desire for order and compulsion for tidiness flaring up. He cringed for a moment, staring at the careless soldier, and then forced his attention back to the screen, making another mental note for later.

"This is fucked," Mills said, staring out the window to the dusty surface beyond. "There's no one left here. Our mission was to find out what happened to comms, and why Earth hadn't heard from these people. I'd say we pretty much completed that mission. They're fucking dead. There is no comms to repair, and even if we did, what the hell good would it do." He turned and walked towards the desk, grabbing the bottle from atop it and shooting a glance to the rep that immediately stifled any objection. He poured a tall glass and walked back to the window, peering back out across the landscape. "I don't know why the hell we're still here."

He'd been quiet since they'd arrived, assessing their situation and preparing mentally for what could happen next. But it was beginning to become a heavy burden on him. He knew that in the grand scheme of things, his rank held about the same weight as the white speck on chicken shit, and with Sarge not around, he felt compelled to vent his opinion.

"Your mission was to accompany myself, a representative of the company that owns this facility, and find out what was going on."

Hawkes turned his attention back to the room. The tone in Talmadge's voice was one he knew was designed to spike a response from Mills. This he inwardly wanted to see. He knew Mills. He was quiet and reserved, but what was hidden behind his zen-like demeanor... He'd been in firefights with him. He knew the anger that bubbled just beneath.

"I'd say we're still doing that," Talmadge continued. "Unless you can explain to the review board back home, a perfectly detailed, scientific explanation of the events that have occurred here."

Mills gritted his teeth, his jaw clenching with the desire to turn and imprint the slimy rep's face into the top of the mahogany desk, another item he knew was on a list of materials no longer legal to possess. But he held his gaze on a cluster of orange rocks a short distance out from the facility, pushing down the urge to snap with another sip of whiskey. Nothing he could say would help with the bureaucratic shitstorm Sarge was already going to have to sit through when he got back. He'd seen it before; politicians, or big company reps dragging even a captain through the mud, leading to a court-martial or being stripped of rank. He wouldn't allow himself to be a reason it could be any worse. So, he bit his tongue, wiped his nose with his hand and took another deep sip of what tasted like it must have been very expensive whiskey. Then he turned around to the sneering gaze of the man at the desk. "I just want to get off this planet as quickly as possible. That's all I'm saying." He downed the rest of the glass and set it on the desk with a heavy thud, turning to make his way past Fascio into the hallway.

"I thought you were gonna put him through the window," Corlin said as he approached.

"And make things even more difficult for Sarge. No... That guys a piece of shit, and there's not a thing that could change that."

"I know something that would," Hawkes said with a grin, reaching out to tap the newly acquired shotgun slung across Fascio's back.

"Shiiiiit. Tempting. Reeeal tempting."

"That's everything," Talmadge said, stepping out from around the desk.

"Then let's get the hell out of here," Mills said, glancing to Hawkes who nodded. "We'll head back to security and regroup there."

Talmadge walked past him as he spoke, his gaze locked to where the hallway curved further down. Fascio shook his head and started to follow when Corlin tapped him on the arm and whispered, "Hold up." He turned and walked quickly back into the room, grabbing the bottle from the desk and jogging back to the others. "Wouldn't wanna leave this. Perfectly good bottle." Fascio smiled, tapping him in the chest and turning to follow the rep back towards security.

"I don't think we're gonna find anything else out right now, Sarge," Vuong said, pulling his eyes form the vidscreen. "There's hundreds of logs. It's gonna take me at least another two hours at this pace." He paused to rub his eyes. They were bloodshot and dry from staring at the monitor and he could feel the distant pulse of a headache beginning just behind them.

"Roger that." Baker clicked open comm. "Alright, marines. Let's pack it in for the night. We'll start fresh in the morning. Regroup at housing in twenty. Portofino, you stay with the bird and make sure nothing happens to her. She's our only ride off this rock."

"Roger that."

"Great," Fascio scoffed as they entered the hallway leading to security and housing. "Just where I wanted to spend the night."

"Come on, Fas," Corlin smiled. "This is a five-star resort. Our own personal pleasure hotel on Mars."

Hawkes took a deep breath and shook his head. Fascio stayed quiet, the striped shirt in the bathtub and smiling face of the boy on the screen flashing past his eyes.

12

Fascio set his tray down on the table across from Vuong and sat down.

"Miss me?" Vuong asked with a smile.

"Like the clap," Fascio replied with a grin as he fanned a plume of stale cigarette smoke away.

A moment later, Lanskey, Dom and Wilkes walked in, making their way to an open table next to theirs. Baker watched as the last of his unit entered, stowed their rifles and freed their heads of their helmets.

Lanskey shook her head as she walked past to the food processors on the wall, telling Sarge with one look that she hadn't found anything new. Sarge nodded, turning his gaze back to the slop on his plate. Then he looked up at Talmadge. "Find everything you were looking for?"

Talmadge nodded as he shoved a spoonful of paste in his mouth, glancing unapprovingly at Fascio who blew another thick cloud of smoke towards the ceiling.

"Good," Sarge said, raising his voice to garner the attention of the others. "Well, the information that Vuong and I have ascertained, is that about three weeks ago, the survey team here on Attis, found a structure that was partially exposed, about three klicks from here. They began excavation on it, and one week ago, for whatever reasons, breached the exterior. Two days later the fine folks here in this complex began to report hearing voices, seeing relatives that had been dead for years, and all manner of other weird shit. Then they decided to start offing themselves, and taking as many others with them as possible. They ran every test imaginable, and came up with nothing. No clue. Which leaves us right here. Now I'm hoping that something on that drive our friend here so desperately needed to acquire can help shed some further light on our current situation." His gaze fell to Talmadge who paused, spoon poised before his mouth.

Talmadge set the spoon down and wiped his lips with a napkin. "The information I retrieved is classified. Only the highest ranking members of the board are entitled to have access to it. Any sharing of this information will lead to immediate court-martial and imprisonment upon returning to Earth. I can't allow—"

"I hope you'll pardon my tone, Talmadge," Baker interrupted. "But I could give a fuck less about your court-martial, or petty threats. People are dead here, and I'm not entirely convinced that the threat has been contained, which means my men here, are now in jeopardy of having the same thing happen to them, and if anything happens to any of my men because you wanna cover your company's ass, or your precious job, and decided that it would be best for you to withhold something that could have potentially avoided it, then I'll be the first to put a bullet between those beady little eyes of yours. So, what do you say you share what's on there with us, or we can take it from you, and lock your ass in one of these perfect, state-of-the-art housing units your company designed until we're ready to leave?"

Wilkes slid his chair out, standing up to move closer to Talmadge.

Talmadge held his seat. He burned within, a fury he was sure he hadn't felt before. His mind was a blur of everything he wanted to do to the sergeant, the things he would do when they returned, but at that moment, everyone's gaze fell upon him, and he knew there was nothing he could do.

'Checkmate.'

Talmadge took a deep breath, reaching into his jacket pocket and pulling the drive out. He set it on the table in front of him and stood, walking out of the room and to one of the units down the hall. His presence there would only serve to get him into a situation that the soldiers could possibly use for leverage, and at the moment, they had nothing on him. His actions were still clean, and in the best interest of the company.

"Well, that's more like it," Baker said, turning his gaze to Vuong. "Let's see what you can get off that."

Vuong nodded, rising from his chair and moving to take the nanodrive. He sat down and pressed a series of buttons on his holowrist. A blue circle illuminated around the drive on the table, and a holographic display of the contents snapped into view; dozens of circular folders containing all the information the facility had procured since inhabitation. The others sat watching as Vuong filtered through the files. After a moment, the screen slowed and he looked up. "I think we have something,

Sarge."

Baker looked at the holographic image of a circular folder with the Xenocorp logo on the front hanging in the air. The words below it read, *AS1.*

"One of the scientists mentioned archeological site one in one of their reports," Vuong said, opening the folder, which fanned out across the space between them.

Pictures and documents hovered in the air, hundreds of each, neatly stacked like a pressed pile of paper. Vuong moved his hand to the photographs and spread his fingers out, fanning the images, which he began to flip through with a wave of his hand. The images were of the surface of the planet, and a small pyramid shape sticking out of the ground. As the pictures flowed past, more and more of the structure was excavated, until the last of the pictures were the pyramid standing nearly three hundred feet deep down into the bottom of the site. The pictures that followed were close-ups of the pyramid's surface. All along the base were inscriptions in what appeared to be a language that none of them had ever seen before. Some of the markings looked almost like those that accompanied the hieroglyphics in ancient Egypt, but the rest were a series of swirls and circular patterns. Vuong flipped through another handful of pictures until they began to show the breach the crew had made into the side. After that were a dozen photographs of a dimly lit tunnel leading inwards. Then the pictures stopped.

"It looks like that's it," Vuong said, turning his gaze to the Sarge. The rest of the group was silent, all contemplating what they had just seen in their own way. "I think maybe we need to see this firsthand," Baker said after a moment, his gaze moving back to the last image of a dark hallway that disappeared into blackness.

"Sarge—" Wilkes began, starting his speech about leaving best alone and how they hadn't been sent there for that.

"We leave at oh' six-hundred," Baker interrupted, ignoring the lance corporal's objection. "Wilkes, you just drew the short straw. You're first up on fire watch. After that I want Fascio, then Mills. Two hour shifts. I'll see you ladies in the morning."

Sarge stood up, making his way out of the room.
"Guess he won't be partaking in any of this then," Hawkes said, smiling as he pulled the bottle of whiskey from his vest and set it on the table.

"Oh, shit," Vuong chuckled. "And just what do we have here?"

"Came across this in the director's office," Hawkes smiled. "Pretty sure he won't mind if we put a little dent in it."

The rest of the unit smiled as he poured himself a glass and passed the bottle around. For the next two hours they were just friends, sitting together chatting over a couple glasses of booze. The facility around them didn't exist, the death and mutilation had faded to the back, and most of the unit didn't even notice the smell that still grew increasingly rank in the halls. They knew it would be there waiting for them in the morning, that there was much more they hadn't even yet to see. But for now, in the chow hall, they were back in their barracks on Earth, sharing stories and reminiscing about the days of past.

Sarge slept peacefully, falling asleep just moments after lying his head on the pillow. It had been some time since he had rested in a bed as comfortable as the one he now lay in. He'd drifted off and now found himself standing in his old house; the one he had lived in before his wife and daughter had been taken from him. The sun was shining brightly through the bedroom window and he could hear light laughter coming from downstairs. *Caroline?* he thought to himself as the vision shifted around him. He started towards the door, his pace quickening as the sound of his daughter giggling fell into his ears. "Moni?" he whispered as the stairs leading to the living room approached. He started down, taking them carefully as a tear began to work its way down his cheek. His heart began to swell in his chest. He kept moving downwards, calling out, "Caroline, Moni?" When he hit the bottom of the stairs he started

121

towards the kitchen, and the sound of their voices. He could feel his pace quickening, his feet moving faster along the carpet. Then he reached the kitchen door and stopped. Spread out in front of him, just inside the doorway, scattered across the black and white linoleum floor were pieces of metal and plastic. He looked up and found himself standing in the middle of an intersection. The street was littered in a sea of broken glass and plastic, which glittered as the midday sun hit against it and he could smell the acrid stench of melted plastic and burnt metal in the air. He slowly stepped forward, recognizing the car that lay upside down, crumpled around the light pole fifty feet away. Another tear fell from his eye. He started towards the wreckage, passing a large truck with its engine sitting where the driver had been moments before, a smoking pile of debris scattered around it. He quickened to a jog, dashing as quickly as he could to the overturned sedan. "Caroline!" he shouted, panic building. "Moni!!" He reached the car and climbed atop it, peering down into the interior from the shattered side window. Lying crumpled within were the still corpses of his wife and daughter, deep gouges running across their flesh, their faces blank and crusted with broken glass, eyes pressed closed. He began to shake, his breath coming in short hitches. He stared downwards, his jaw quivering as silent lips formed their names. Then a freezing chill ran across his back and his wife's eyes shot open.

Sergeant Thomas awoke with a start, salted rivulets down his cheeks as new tears still formed along his eyes. He swallowed hard, peering into the black of the room as his eyes adjusted; the only light coming from a dim overhead that illuminated just enough to see through the darkness. Sweat held his shirt tightly to him, moisture warped with sadness and anguish clinging wetly. As he brought his hands up to wipe the tears away he saw Corlin on the bed across from him. The corporal was silent, staring blankly across the room at a closet that had been left open. He watched him for a moment, the man's eyes unblinking as his blank gaze peered into the open portal. Another feeling moved in, pressing the sadness to the darkness behind him as it took hold.

"Everything all right?" he asked, his own gaze moving to the empty closet he had cleared when he first entered the room. The other man didn't respond, didn't even break his gaze to acknowledge him. The feeling grew, festering deep in his chest. "Corlin, I asked you if everything is fine," he repeated. Still no response. "Corporal!" he barked, causing Fascio to lift his head from the pillow on the floor to look at him at the outburst.

Corlin slowly turned his gaze to the sergeant. He blinked twice and nodded in the dark. "Sorry, Sarge," he whispered, his voice dry and cracked. "Thought I saw something."

Baker stared at him for a moment before the other man looked at the closet again and then lay back down in his bed without explanation. Fascio glanced up at him and nodded, a silent question, asking if everything was all right. Baker felt his stomach tighten, the unmistakable cue that something wasn't right. For the next twenty minutes he lay there doing his best to analyze their situation and processing everything he had seen. But eventually his thoughts went back to his dream, and the family he would never go home to again. As he lay there, anxiously waiting for sleep to once again pull him away, he brought his hands up to the sides of his head. He'd had the onset of a migraine since that afternoon, and as he lay on his back, he could feel his pulse pounding behind his temples. The pain was getting worse, and he knew the first thing he was going to do when he woke up was chase his breakfast with a handful of Aspirin.

13

"You have the coordinates?" Sarge asked, his spoon piercing into a pile of what was supposed to taste like eggs and cheese.

"Affirm, Sarge," Vuong replied, taking a sip out of a glass of processed orange beverage. "Three klicks northwest. Should be there in less than ten if the rovers are operational. An hour or so on foot."

"I believe this is yours," Baker said, sliding the nanodrive across the table at Talmadge who had quietly taken a seat and was eating silently, avoiding conversation with the rest. "And we're gonna do you one even better. You're gonna get to inspect your alien structure firsthand. We head out in fifteen. We're gonna go check it out ourselves and see if we can figure out what the hell it was that they found in there, since apparently there's nothing on that little drive of yours about it."

Talmadge stared at the drive for a moment before reaching out to pick it up. He kept his gaze at the table and slid the drive into his vest pocket, then continued eating in silence. He knew there would be no way they could have found, let alone accessed the encrypted files hidden away. Only the terminals back on Earth could open them.

Baker stared at the man who was usually quick to snap and assert his authority. There were dark circles puffed out beneath his eyes and he could see the two-day stubble scruffed across his chin. He could see that the man hadn't slept very well the night before, but hell, he thought to himself, which of them had...? The thought that almost brought a grin to his face was that he knew Talmadge was a clean-cut, corporate man, and that it had to be eating him alive to allow himself to go so long without a shower and a shave. An old quip ran through his mind as he pulled his glance away. It truly was the little things.

When they had finished eating they suited up and started their way back to the main landing pad, and the two rovers they had passed on the way in. The odor in the facility had become noticeably worse overnight, and two of the men, and Lanskey, had tied cloth around their faces to block out the assaulting stench. They made their way back past communications and admitting, pausing as they approached the main airlock. It seemed that having the smell accompanying the sight only served to make the situation seem even worse.

"We do this by the numbers," Baker said, bringing all focus to him. "We go out there, see whatever the hell it is we can find, and then we get back here on the double. Now, I know some of you are thinking, this isn't our mission, and that this isn't what we are here for, but the fact is, we are here, and there is no one else that can find out what happened to these poor bastards, so that objective now falls on us. We're still awaiting reply from base, so until we get orders otherwise, we're stuck here, so suck it up. We're E.M.F., and I'm not worried about some stupid colonist with a wrench taking any of us out, are you?"

"Ooh-rah!"

"Good. Then suit up, and let's see what these poor bastards unearthed out there."

The unit engaged their envirosuits, freeing them from the pack on their belts, and pulling them around their arms and legs. When they were clasped at the top of the neck, the suit did the rest, sealing down the back, and fusing every seam. The sleeves sealed to the gloves and the neck to their helmet. In moments, the group was suited up and standing in the airlock.

"Let's take a walk," Sarge said, nodding to Vuong who engaged the outer door, venting the atmosphere and putting the transport ship into view.

"Portofino," Sarge said as they made their way to the nearest rover. "Good to go?"

"Read you loud and clear Sarge, over."

"We're gonna take ourselves a little field trip. I need you to stay by that radio, and be ready for evac should we find ourselves needing extraction."

"Roger that, Sarge. Ready and waiting."

"Just like I like 'em," Dom clicked across, eliciting a smile and a fist pound from Fascio.

"We know how you like them Dom," Hawkes clicked across. "Ruffied and young."

"Just the male ones though," Mills added with a smile.

"Alright, ladies, that's enough."

The unit approached the rover. It was a ten-person transport unit that had run flat tires and a suspension equipped for travel across the martian terrain. As they approached, Baker found himself wondering why in the last two hundred years of technological advances, with the colonization of the moon and deep space travel now commonplace, that the planetary rovers still had the same design as the ones they used on the first visit to the moon over a century ago; a bulky steel frame with exposed seats, no wind screen and comfort the last thing in mind when designed. He let his gaze fall to the landscape beyond, the tingle of exhilaration passing quickly through him. Again, he found himself doing something he never thought he would. Another reminder why he had joined the corps, another distraction.

To say the ride across the surface to the site was bumpy, would have been like saying that someone at the facility had simply passed away. The marines were jerked back and forth, their internal organs ricocheting off each other, every muscle tense in an attempt to hold their body together. The landscape had always looked relatively smooth in photographs, but as they bounced along, they could see that it was anything other than that. They were halfway there when Wilkes yelled across the comms, "I think I might actually enjoy flying more than this."

"This is worse than those BS-thirty-twos we were crammed in in Africa," Fascio yelled back against the roar of the rover's engine.

"Yeah," Vuong shouted. "But you might not catch gonorrhea here."

"Hey, man, how the hell was I supposed to know she was a hooker?"

"Maybe because she slept with you..?"

"You got a good point there," Wilkes shouted back with a smile.

"You might wanna leave your mother out of this," Fascio shouted, taking one hand of the seat handles to flip him off."

"Sarge."

Baker looked up to Vuong who was driving. The soldier was pointing out in front. He let his eyes trace the imaginary line, and then saw what the other was showing him. Barely visible against the endless sea of red and orange, stood a small gray object that stood at a point along the horizon.

"That's gotta be it," Vuong shouted, the image on his holowrist confirming the location.

"Bring us as close as possible," Baker shouted, his gaze not falling from the structure that was growing closer. Ten minutes later they were stopped at the edge of a circular pit that led down to the base of the giant pyramid.

The unit stepped out, making their way to the edge and peered down. Before them stood a structure slightly smaller than the pyramids in Egypt, but with sides that were constructed out of what appeared to be some type of metallic material. It was a dull grey and smooth to a polish, the top of the structure coming together in a point that looked almost needle sharp. There were engravings along the base that seemed to almost glow an iridescent-blue color, standing out brightly against the dark surface and they could see the circular rings surrounding it where vehicles had been used to remove the Earth it was buried beneath.

"What do you think, Sarge?" Wilkes asked, his gaze locked to the alien construct.

"Let's go see what all the fuss is about shall we?" Baker scanned the space below, seeing where the excavation road reached the top a short distance away. "Brass check, I don't want any mistakes. You pull that shit you did in medical again, Dom..."

"I know Sarge, I'll be walking home."

"Good," Baker said, turning to eye his unit. "Then what are we standing around for, we've got ourselves an alien structure to go inspect."

The others turned and followed him to the road leading downwards. They followed it for nearly an hour as it circled around and around the pyramid, finally coming to a basin at the bottom.

They made their way to where the original excavation team had breached the structure walls. There was an opening blown into the side a short distance away and they stopped just in front of it. Around them, red walls layered upwards until all that was visible beyond was the swirl of an orange sky.

"Lights up, everyone. Fascio, you're on point, Dom, Corlin, after him. Mills, Hawkes, you follow us up.

Everybody, stay together. We don't know what's in there.

"Doc, you're with me."

14

The structure's interior was absolute blackness—deeper than the void outside, more suffocating than the grave. The air was thick, pressing in from all sides, swallowing the weak beams of helmet and rifle lights, choking them down until the illumination seemed to die before it could reach the walls. Every breath felt heavy, as if the atmosphere itself was resisting their intrusion, clinging to their suits and seeping into their lungs.

The hallway was a corridor of polished, seamless metal, stretching endlessly into the dark. Their footsteps echoed hollow and uncertain, each sound devoured by the oppressive silence. The path ahead vanished into a tunnel that seemed to consume light, a passage that threatened to swallow them whole.

For ten agonizing minutes, they moved deeper, the blackness growing thicker, the sense of being watched intensifying with every step. The air felt colder, heavier, as if something ancient and malevolent was lurking just beyond the reach of their lights, waiting for them to falter.

Finally, they reached an intersection—the first sign that the tunnel did not stretch on forever into oblivion. The corridors to the left and right disappeared into the same suffocating dark, but ahead,

Baker thought he saw it: a faint, sickly glow, barely more than a whisper of light, flickering in the distance like a dying ember.

He raised his hand, voice low and tense. "Everybody hold." The unit froze, breath caught in their throats, the silence pressing in. "I want everyone to go dark."

For a moment, the only sound was the pounding of their hearts, the blackness around them alive, hungry, and waiting.

"What was that, Sarge?" Fascio asked, not sure what the sergeant meant.

"Lights out, everyone," he clarified, reaching up to kill his helmet light.

"Are you sure this is such a good idea?" Dom asked, the others already following the sergeant's order.

"This is not a discussion."

Dom took a deep breath and clicked his rifle light off, mumbling about how he wished they had their NVG's as he reached up to kill the one on his helmet. Instantly the group was standing in complete darkness; pitch black that only left phantom traces of shapes shifting in front of their eyes as they squinted into the nothingness beyond.

"There," Baker whispered through the comms.
"Twelve o'clock. Does that look like a light to you?"
Fascio squinted hard against the dark, allowing his eyes to adjust. Then he saw what Sarge was talking about. Far down the corridor ahead

was a faint glow, almost unnoticeable; a trick playing off the dancing spots in his vision.

"I don't know how you caught that, Sarge," Fascio replied, "but yeah, I think it is."

"Lights up. Looks like we found our direction."

The soldiers quickly brought their lights back to life, pushing back the blackness as they started forward, their hands not pressing the switches nearly fast enough. Baker could feel the same scraping sensation as in the facility, but here, surrounded by the claustrophobic dark, the eyes in the black seemed to peer past his soul. He could feel the cold working through him as he made his way further in, his companions nearly becoming a vacant thought as his gaze watched the approaching glow brighten in the hall. It was minutes later that the illumination became decipherable, the patterns casting off the azure glow becoming visible across the walls.

As they approached, they realized that it was the same inscriptions from the outside of the structure, some form of bio or chemical-luminescence causing them to glow. Vuong brought his hand up to brush the surface, and in that moment, Fascio shot his hand out, grabbing his arm.

"Whoa," Fascio whispered.

Vuong glanced at him for a moment and then pulled his arm back.

"It's cool, man."

Vuong brought his hand up, sliding his glove against the ancient surface. The runes on the wall were smooth. There was no imprint, no bevel, they seemed as if they were part of the wall itself. He stared at the shapes, the light casting its glow across his features. He was fixated, the ebbing azure sending a chill through him like an icy breath of wind. "It's smooth."

"I didn't see any pictures of this on that drive," Baker said, observing the hieroglyphs that stretched farther towards the center of the structure. "You wanna catch this?" he asked, turning to look at Talmadge. "I think your higher-ups might be interested in seeing this, don't you think? Who knows, might even get you a raise." This was his attempt at being civil, though the moment the words finished leaving his lips he felt a ping of embarrassment at coming off as what could be construed as a kiss-ass.

Talmadge held quiet, reaching up to his helmet to engage the camera function. He hadn't thought about it until this moment, and for a fleeting breath, was thankful that the sergeant reminded him. But that would still hold no bearing against the fact he was going to drag his ass through the mud when they got back home. Hopefully, he would do something stupid now that he was on camera, something that could bolster his case against him. Though smiling inwardly, he knew it wouldn't take much to turn the whole situation around and place the blame for the events all on Thomas's head. He turned and nodded, flashing his best pseudo-camaraderie.

Baker waited long enough for the rep to snap a few stills and then turned to continue inward. The symbols bore into him as he passed, tiny ripples spreading their way out across his back as he continued. He could feel the hallway closing in and the pressure building behind his eyes as the headache that had yet to dissipate continued to grow. Then a tickle brushed past his ear, a touch of warmth guided by phantom breath.

*"We're here."*

Baker stopped, his feet frozen in place as the men behind him came to a halt. He brought his hand up to his helmet, his fingers pressing against the spot the soft words had just come from. Slowly he turned, his pupils locking to the first face that fell into view.

"You okay, Sarge?" Mills asked, seeing the brief look of panic in his sergeant's eyes.

He stared at the marine for a moment before replying slowly. "Yeah." His gaze moved to the darkness behind the others, locking to the void that pressed in on them. "Just thought I heard something."

"Like what, Sarge?" Mills asked, his brow wrinkling beneath his helmet.

"I don't know," Baker replied, glancing into the dark one last time before turning around and following the others. "Something. Maybe nothing. Let's keep moving."

He turned and continued onwards, allowing two of the others to move forward while he fell back. Ice still ran frozen through his veins as he fell into pace just behind Lanskey. He grasped desperately at some semblance of sanity as his wife's breath still lingered strong inside his helmet. Gooseflesh beneath his uniform held his skin tight against his frame and he could feel the moisture clamming up his hands. He kept silent as they continued forward, pushing her voice from his head, and convincing himself that he had hallucinated it, that it wasn't real. His head still hurt and he could feel the pounding getting worse. He just had to keep it together. They would find out what the colonists had found, or at least the remnants of it, and then they would get back to the safety of the facility. He scoffed silently at the thought that the word safety had even crossed his mind when thinking about the station, but in contrast with how he felt at the current moment, he would be glad to be back there as quickly as possible. He could only assume the others felt the same way.

The unit moved further in, a short time later coming to another intersection. The hall they had been following intersected with another corridor that disappeared on both sides further into the structure. In front of them was another portal cut into the wall. Baker scanned the rubble with his flashlight, noticing the scorch marks along the edges where a very powerful mining torch had ripped through the walls material. "Vuong?" Baker clicked across the comm. "Was there any schematic on that drive?"

Vuong fired up his holowrist, flipping through the files, flashing light bouncing across the smooth surface around them. A moment later he stopped, expanding an image into the air in front of him. "Got it, Sarge," he said, pausing as he looked at it closer. "Strange though. Not a lot to see. Single corridor running just inside the perimeter, single one running to the center, and the one we're standing in circling a tight perimeter around a central room with no connection to the outer."

Baker inspected the image closer, a thousand questions firing off in his mind like bells in an ancient steeple.

"Why is this here?" Vuong whispered, asking one of the questions lingering in Baker's thoughts.

"You're right," he continued, pointing at the holoimage. "The hallway on the outside connects to the inner one, but nowhere is there a connection to the center room. No doorway, nothing. From an engineering standpoint, whoever built this didn't want anyone even knowing it was there. If I had to guess, I'd say this structure was designed to hide whatever was in that room." He scoffed. "Whoever it was that built this, went through a lot of trouble not only coming to Mars , but building an entire pyramid around a sealed room, and then burying it beneath the surface. So, my question, is what the hell did those colonists find in there?"

"Whatever," Dom whispered, his gaze glued to the image.

"What?" Vuong replied, looking at him puzzled.

"*What* ever built this...."

"Yeah," Vuong whispered into the comm. "And I'm not sure it's exactly something we should be looking for?"

A ripple of murmured nervousness flashed through the group as each of them exchanged worried glances.

Baker allowed the comment to pass unchecked. He knew they were scared. Hell, no more than he was. And at the moment he was too preoccupied with his own unspoken questions. Every fiber of his being told him that his next move was a bad idea, but his entire career was hosted on nothing but, so pushed the feeling back and readied himself to add another tally to his marks. Slowly he turned his flashlight and scanned the inside of the room, sweeping as much as he could before making the even worse decision to step in. Beyond the scorched edges lay a bare room, twelve foot across and eight feet high. The walls inside were covered in inscriptions similar to those on the hallways and surface of the structure, but these ones were carved deeply into the walls, gouged into the foreign material, floor to ceiling. Along the base were small, neat piles of a black material so dark that it seemed to absorb the light from Baker's flashlight as it moved across it, yet at the same time, sparkled lightly. The cell was an empty void. "Well, whatever it was, it's not here now."

Baker felt a chill move past him, an icy mist unseen that frosted his skin for a moment, leaving the hairs on his arms and neck standing at attention. He shuddered for a moment, deep fears rising up as he turned to the others. "Sarge, you know I'm not one to complain, but this place is starting to freak me out. I really don't think we should be here."

Baker stared at the man who until this moment, had been one of the most reserved, serious soldiers in his unit. He took a deep breath and glanced back into the room for a moment.

"It doesn't look like there's anything else to see here. Let's start making our way back."

He agreed with Corlin, there was something ripping at him, tearing desperately inside him to turn and run. Whatever had been inside the empty room had been removed by the colonists, and there was no mention of it in any of the files. Whatever they found was either long gone, or still hidden somewhere in the facility. The only thing he knew for sure at that moment, was that his men were right. They needed to get back. There was nothing they were going to be able to do except waste the air in their tanks. As he turned to step out of the room the thought flashed past his mind. What if the room was empty, not because something had been removed, but because whatever it had housed, had simply been freed.

The others nodded, turning to make their way back down the long hallway to the entrance, their steps coming noticeably quicker now. Each of them held their fear behind their masked visors. None of them wanted to be there a moment longer than they had to, and if it wasn't for Sarge keeping the pace, every one of them would have launched into a full sprint.

"Portofino, any response from HQ? Over."
Nothing came back, not even static. The comms were as dead and black as the corridor that enveloped them. "Portofino," Baker repeated, "Are you reading me?" Nothing.

"Shit."
"Some kind of interference," Vuong replied. "Picked it up when we first made our way in. There's something keeping radio signals from coming in or going out. Even the holowrist is acting a little funny. Probably whatever material this thing's made out of is jamming us."

Baker held his response. He could still feel the chill worming through him, and was anxious to get back to the facility so he could free himself of his envirosuit. It felt like it was holding the cold in, like it was swirling around him, leeching his strength as he continued outwards. Beneath the helmet, his head was still pounding, the rhythmic pulses crescendoing harder and higher every step he took. The first thing he was going to do when they got back was down a half a bottle of aspirin, chased with some of the whiskey he had heard his men speaking about. If it wasn't for having to maintain composure, he would have turned to a sprint a long time ago.

The unit made their way back towards the entrance, and had been walking quietly for ten minutes when something brushed past Corlin's ear; a faint whisper coming from behind him. Immediately he turned his head, his pace slowing to a stop as he stared into the darkness he had just traveled. As the others continued forward, their lights slowly dimming with each step further from him they became, he paused. He moved his light further down the hall and then froze, the hairs at the nape of his neck rippling with an unseen chill.

"What...?"

Standing just at the edge of his gun's light was a young girl. She was no more than ten years old, with dirty blond hair hanging in strands around her shoulders. She was wearing dirty colonial clothing and had a makeshift breathing apparatus strapped around her head. Her light blue eyes stared at him pleadingly beneath the mask.

"Please," she whispered, her voice crackling across his comms with an electric buzz layered behind it. "Please help." Her arms folded across her stomach as she slowly folded in on herself.

"Sarge!" Corlin snapped through the comms as the girl began stepping backwards towards the center of the structure, her gaze locked firmly to his. "We've got a live one!" Corlin glanced back to the others and saw them stop.

"Roger that," Baker snapped back. "Retrieve her."

"On it," Corlin replied, turning to look back at the empty space the girl had just been standing in. "Hey, wait!" Corlin flashed his light down the corridor. The girl was gone. "Damn," he grumbled to himself, starting his way quickly down the hall.

The unit was nearly to the entrance when Hawkes turned his head to scan the hall behind them. He'd felt eyes watching him from the moment they left the room in the center. Every step he took felt as though they were being stalked, and he had forced himself to keep his eyes forward until the light from the entrance was in view. Now he grappled the courage to look. "Sarge," he snapped, stopping in place. "Corlin's gone."

Baker stopped in his tracks, turning to look where Hawkes was standing. "Corlin," he barked across the comm. "Do you read me? What's your twenty?" Silence replied over the headset. "Corlin god damnit, where are you?"

Still silence.

A cold foreboding worked through him. In a breath he was overcome by the feeling that something had gone horribly wrong. His unit knew better than to go off on their own. They moved as a team, though some of them bordered on the verge of insubordination at times, none of them would make a decision without running it by him. No. Something had happened. He could feel it. "He was right behind us when we left, Sarge," Hawkes replied, his flashlight scanning back down the corridor. A thin layer of worry lingered around his words.

"Corlin!" Sarge exhaled heavily. "God damnit. Fuck. All right. We backtrack. Maybe his comms set is acting up. If what Vuong said is true, then this structure is affecting our electronics. Let's go find the Corporal."

The group turned around and reluctantly started making their way back down the corridor, each of them whispering their own silent curses.

"I don't like this Sarge," Fascio clicked a minute later. "Something ain't right. Corlin wouldn't just go AWOL. That ain't like him. He would have said something."

Baker stayed quiet. Fascio was right. Corlin was by the books. He was the one in his unit that wouldn't even go piss without asking permission to release stream.

"We shouldn't have come out here..."
"Stow it, Fascio," Baker growled, his rifle illuminating the hallway a short distance away.

Corlin moved through the corridor, the runes that had glowed moments before now vanished, swallowed by the metallic gloom. The silence was suffocating, broken only by the echo of his own footsteps. He felt the oppressive weight of the structure pressing in, the darkness thickening with every step. It was as if the walls themselves were watching, waiting for something to happen.

He hadn't gone far before she appeared—a pale, fragile shape hunched against the back wall of the central room. The air seemed to freeze around her, and Corlin's breath caught in his throat. He swept his light across the space, the beam trembling in his grip. "I got her," he whispered into the comm, his voice barely audible.

As he approached, the girl didn't move. Her face was buried in her arms, her shoulders shaking with heavy, shuddering breaths. The chill in the room deepened, crawling up Corlin's spine and settling in his bones. "It's okay," he said softly, slinging his rifle behind his back, forcing calm into his voice. "We're here to help. We're with the military. We're going to get you out of here."

The girl's breathing slowed, but she remained motionless. The only sound was the static buzz in Corlin's helmet, growing louder, drowning out his thoughts. The cold pressed in, numbing his senses. Then, in a voice that seemed to vibrate through the air, she whispered, "I can't leave. We can't leave."

Corlin hesitated, the dread clawing at his insides. "Why not?" he managed, taking another step closer. The temperature seemed to drop, the darkness thickening, pressing against his skin.

"I'm too weak. I'm not ready yet," she replied, her words heavy, each syllable buzzing in his ears.

Corlin tried to reassure her, his voice trembling. "We're going to help you, okay?" He closed the distance, his legs moving on their own, until he was right behind her.

Suddenly, the static in his head surged, a cacophony of noise and pressure that forced his eyes wide. The cold was absolute, suffocating, and all other sensations faded away.

"Yes. You will," the girl said, turning her face toward him.

Corlin's scream tore through the silence as he stared at her face—her mask gone, skin shredded in deep, ragged gashes from scalp to chin, as if she had tried to claw her own face away. Where her eyes should have been, two blood-soaked hollows stared back, black voids gouged deep into her skull. She rose slowly, her movements unnatural, and reached out with tiny, ruined hands.

The silence swallowed his screams, leaving only the echo of terror reverberating in the frozen air.

The group rushed down the corridor, back towards the central room. Baker called out across the comms again. "Corlin, do you read me?"

No sooner had his words left the comm, then he saw the corporal standing a short distance down the hall. "What in the hell are you thinking, Corporal?" Baker asked as they approached, "Are you trying to piss me off?"

As the group got closer, light illuminated his features, a look beyond panic and fear warping his face beneath his helmet.

"Corlin?" Hawkes asked, the look on his friend's face slowly registering. "What's wrong, man?" The others came to a staggered halt.

Corlin was shaking visibly, his body wracked with tremors, his breath coming in short, hyperventilated gasps. His eyes darted between them like a mouse backed into a corner by a pack of starving cats and they could see his hands balled into tight fists at his side. Behind him, invisible to the others, the tiny girl stood, her blackened portals fixed to his back. Now his voice came through over the comms.

"We can't leave," he whispered, his voice now crackling across. "I can't leave. None of us can." His voice broke. "We can't." Tears began to work their way down his cheeks.

"Corporal," Baker whispered, his hands raising slowly in the air. "We're right here. Ain't nobody getting left behind. You're gonna be fine, and we are all gonna leave here together, alright?" He took a step closer when the other man quickly pulled his sidearm and leveled it at him.

Baker noticed in an instant how sloppy the motion was, and how bad the man's hands were shaking behind it. There was no training in the corporal's form. Another sign that didn't sit well. He could have drawn, disassembled and reassembled his pistol in a coma without a second lapse.

"Corporal, you lower that weapon. You hear me?
That's an order, Marine." His words were soft and steady.
The girl slowly reached out, her fingers wrapping around the belt at his back.

"I can't. If it gets back…"
"If what gets back, Son?" Baker asked as Corlin's sentence trailed off, his eyes still shooting wildly between the group. "If what gets back?"

*Ssshhhhhh*
Corlin's mind was a storm of fractured memories and intrusive shadows, reality unraveling as the darkness pressed in. Thoughts slipped through his grasp, each one blending with the next until he could no longer tell what was his and what was conjured by the thing lurking just behind him. The world felt unreal, dreamlike, yet every sensation was painfully sharp. "It can't," he whispered, the words barely his own.

In a sudden, desperate motion, Corlin reached down and disengaged his envirosuit. The oxygen vented in a violent hiss, cold air biting at his skin.

148

"Corlin!" Hawkes shouted, lunging toward him—but in a blur, Corlin raised his sidearm to his head.

Tears streamed from bloodshot eyes as his mouth opened and closed, gulping the thin Martian air that burned his lungs. Desperation twisted his features, a silent plea for help flickering in his gaze. Then, with a trembling finger, he pulled the trigger.

The report echoed down the corridor, and Baker flinched as the corporal's blood splattered across the wall. Corlin's body crumpled, lifeless, to the floor.

"No!" Hawkes screamed, anguish dousing his words.
"FUCK!!!!"
"What the fuck!!?" Vuong shouted.
A frenzy of hysteria wracked the group.
"I fucking told you we shouldn't have come here," Fascio said, turning to pace back and forth behind them.

"I fucking told you!"
Baker stared blankly at the man who had minutes ago been talking lively amongst them, who less than an hour prior had sat across from him on the rover, gazing across the planet's landscape. His mind raced, a jumble of senseless thoughts all twisting together into a vortex of fear and anguish.

"What the fuck is going on Sarge?" Mills clicked, snapping Baker back to the group that was grasping at any semblance of composure. The problem was, this time he didn't have any of the answers they were looking for. This time he was simply just another marine.

Baker's mind raced, the vision of Corlin standing before him burned into his vision. His training told him to speak up, to direct his men and create order out of the chaos that had exploded around them, but his instincts pulled him in on himself. He stood frozen as the others shouted questions to each other and waved their rifle lights back and forth in the hall. He let his gaze fall to Corlin's still twitching corpse and realized that he had been holding his breath.

"Fascio, Mills, you carry Corlin," he said softly while exhaling heavily. "We're getting the hell out of here. Everyone stays together, no one strays. We move two by two and I want clear line of sight on everyone. Now let's move, double time."

The men picked up Corlin's corpse and started down the hallway with the others. They were walking as quickly as they could without tripping over their feet in the dark, their headlamps bobbing wildly as they made their way towards the exit. What they had just seen left a cold space within them deeper than the air that warped around them. None of them spoke a word until they were back on the rover and the Attis station was falling back into view.

"What happened in there Sarge?" Fascio asked, his gaze falling hard across to Baker.

"I have no idea," Baker replied, glancing down to where Corlin lay covered in a tarp at their feet. "He must have been compromised; affected by whatever it was that caused it to happen to the people in Attis."

Beneath them the rover bounced unfazed along the rocky landscape.

"But we all had our envirosuits on," Vuong replied. "Why was it just him?"

Again, Baker found himself falling short of answers, a feeling he was slowly realizing he wasn't comfortable getting used to.

"Maybe somehow, he got himself infected before we went out."

"It's not an infection," Lanskey said, bringing their eyes to her. She shook her head slowly while bouncing in uncomfortably hard seat. "All pathology reads normal, toxicology as well. This is something else. I think this is psychological. Possibly, even xenomorphic in nature."

The group held silent as the rovers engine growled, a large bump lurching them sideways.

"What," Fascio asked a moment later as his brow scrunched together tightly behind his mask. "Like some kind of alien?"

"That's what I'm hoping to find out."

"Well, if it is alien," Baker growled, "Then that means it's alive, which also means it can be killed. And if that's the case, then we're gonna do what we do best, and blow it the hell back to wherever it is that it came from."

"And how do you suppose you're going to do that, Sergeant," Talmadge asked, his gaze locked to Baker from across the rover. "You don't even know what *it* is."

Baker looked up at the rep, his gaze stabbing through the space between them. "I know two things, Talmadge. First, I know that whatever it is that's causing this, was released because of your precious company, and the moment we get back to Earth, every organization and media outlet on the planet is going to know that you assholes are personally responsible for the deaths of every single person in this colony, as well as one of the marines sent to accompany you on your cover up mission. And secondly, we're marines! We'll figure it out. That's what we do. We fight, we kill, and we survive. And I'll be God damned, if I survived six tours and a world war, to come have my ass taken out by some god damned bug." Baker turned to the others, his gaze scanning each of their faces as he raised his voice above the rover's engine. "From now on, nobody goes anywhere alone. We travel in teams, no less than two, and if any of us start acting funny, the others will immediately relieve them of their weapons, no hesitation, and we will slap their asses right back into reality. Does everyone understand?"

The group nodded. "Rah. Roger that."

"The second we're back," he continued, pointing at Vuong and Fascio, "I want the two of you back in security. You keep looking until you find something. We need to figure out what the hell it was that killed those colonists, and what it is that has now taken a liking to marine blood.

We're up against something here, and it's not stupid. We need to know what the hell it is, and how we can kill it before any more of us depart this shit life we've been given." He paused, looking to Dom who sat uncharacteristically quiet. "You and Wilkes will accompany Lanskey back to medical the moment we return. I wanna know every symptom that's been recorded from the moment they returned from that thing, and I want psych profiles on every colonist. Look for patterns in behavior leading up to death and the patterns of the deaths themselves. If something is killing us, or getting us to punch our own clocks, then I want to know how it is that it's doing it. I wanna know how it hunts, what it wants, how it gets into our heads, everything. If we're all hearing voices, then they have to be coming from somewhere, and it's only safe to assume that it's whatever is causing all this. The rest of us are going to make our way back to the facility director's room, and we're going to have a nice little conversation about the clusterfuck this facility has become. Then we're gonna dig so deep into that computer, we're gonna need a rope and harness to climb back out."

"Sergeant Thomas, I can't—"

"Shut the fuck up, Talmadge! One of my men are dead, because of your fuck up. You're about this close from being next." He held up his middle finger and gritted his teeth together, turning his gaze back to Vuong. "The second you find out anything."

"You got it, Sarge."

Baker turned his gaze to the facility looming closer. Before he had gone into the pyramid he had been upset, disturbed and bordering distressed. Now he was angry, violently vehement. Whatever it was that had killed the people in the facility, now had his men in its crosshairs, which meant that it wasn't some virus, or flu. It was intelligent, picking them off one by one, separating them from the pack when they were their weakest. That meant it was sentient, which also meant that it could be killed. This thing wanted war... and killing one of his men was the quickest way it could have gotten it. Sergeant Thomas's original intention had been to wait for reply from HQ and then comply with whatever those instructions would be. Now, that was piss spray in the wind. There was no standing by, no waiting for proper channels. He was gonna find this thing, and he was gonna kill it, and none of them were going to leave until he was damn sure whatever it was that killed Corporal John Corlin was good and dead.

15

A solemn distance hung between the unit as they made their way back into the facility. Heavy was the loss bore from the shattered camaraderie. Silence clung to them, their words stifled by a sadness that built in the form of tears at the edge of their eyes. They had all known Corlin for a long time. He was part of their family, a friend and brother, and now, with no way to stop it, and helpless to intervene, he was dead, taken out by his own hand.

Nothing about it made sense. Nothing.

They made their way back towards security, passing admissions down the hallway that led to environmental. The smell in the station had grown violently pungent in places, the primary airlock and entrance to admissions the worst. The filtration system struggled to keep up with the clouding odor, but with so many sources, it made for an impossible task. They had dragged some of the bodies onto the landing pad when they first made their way in, a minute attempt to quell the rising stench, but the smell was already one that none of them would be purging any time soon.

As they approached the entrance to the corporate offices, Baker stopped, glancing to Vuong and Fascio. "The moment you find anything."

"On it, Sarge," Fascio replied, tapping Vuong on the shoulder as he turned to make his way back to security, Wilkes, Dom and Lanskey following along. "Let's go see what the fuck killed Corlin," he said, shooting a stern glance to Talmadge and turning to make his way past reception.

Vuong and Fascio were in the lead of the group, walking quietly when the lights above began to flicker, dimming to the point of blackness before snapping back to life. The throbbing illumination added to the façade that the facility was sentient and ever monitoring.

"I'm really beginning to hate this place," Fascio said, his rifle shifting in his grip.

"Yeah," Vuong replied, squinting into the hallway ahead. "I'm gonna be taking a long leave when I get back, and I'm putting in for transfer. I can't do this space shit any more..."

"I'll be standing in line next to you, buddy," Fascio replied. "I think this was it for me too. I'd rather dodge bullets back home than ever have to go through something like this again. Resources or not, I'm never leaving Los Angeles. I don't care if it is a hundred and twenty, year-round. Fuck space." "Amen to that."

They reached security and turned to the others. "If you need anything," Fascio said, turning to Wilkes. "We're right down the hall."

"Roger that, Fas," Wilkes replied, reaching out to clasp his hand firmly.

"You be careful."
"Ooh-Rah."

Wilkes nodded, releasing his grasp on Fascio's hand to step back and look at Dom and Lanskey. "Let's get to medical. I wanna know what the hell it is we're fighting here."

Dom nodded, extending his hand for Wilkes to lead the way.

Back in administrations, Baker, Talmadge and Hawkes were just approaching the director's office. The lights in the hallway had failed, leaving only the emergency overheads. As they made their way into the room, Baker broke the silence that had accompanied them from the moment they had passed reception.

"Go ahead and pull up everything you can find. I want to know what they found out there, what they brought back, and the names of the men that did. I want pictures, samples and anything else that might help us." He stared at Talmadge, waiting for him to move to the computer. "Now," he growled, his patience stretched to its last strand. "Vuong," he clicked across. "You and Fascio back at security yet?"

"That's affirmative," Vuong clicked back.

"Good. Slight change of plans. I want you to pull up full schematics of the facility. I want every door not in our immediate path sealed, full override on the locks. I don't want anything coming in or out of even so much as a ventilation duct. Seal off everything. Let me know when it's done."

"Ten-four," Vuong replied, turning to the monitor and bringing the station plans to life.

Talmadge sat at the desk, Baker standing just behind him as he poured through the sealed reports surrounding the excavation. He had found the names of the survey crew that had found it, and the ones that breached the exterior and inner walls. Lightly, he skimmed the tip of the classified section, showing just enough to quell the sergeant's need for answers. The crew had recorded everything, documenting the runes script, maps of the interior and even collected samples of the material the structure was comprised of, which the science department had returned as previously unclassified and foreign in composition. They reported breaching the inner wall, and every one of their statements was the same; the wall fractured and as soon as the section cut fell away, they were hit with a freezing cold that seemed to move through them. It was accompanied by a feeling of panic; a fear none of them had ever felt before. One of the men had thrown up and passed out on the spot, another turned and ran from the facility, and was found nearly ten miles away, wandering the martian landscape, mumbling incoherently. That colonist in particular had been brought back to the facility and placed in the infirmary. He had secluded to a semi-catatonic state, where he would go into fits of extreme emotion, violently angry one moment, and crying hysterically another. The reports said that nothing had been found in the center chamber, that everything was kept exactly as it was, being left for an archeological crew that was set to arrive at Attis later.

Baker processed the information as quickly as it appeared across the screen.

"So, they didn't find anything inside the pyramid?" Hawkes asked from over his shoulder.

"It would appear that way," Baker replied. "Or whatever it was they found, they just didn't see, or it escaped as they were breaching the room."

"Then it's safe to assume, that the structure they uncovered, had absolutely nothing to do with what happened here at all, that it was something else, maybe a freak psychological phenomenon that caused some of the colonists to go on a killing spree." Talmadge moved the files to the recycle bin, his words covering his actions.

Baker looked at Talmadge who held his gaze at the monitor.

"Freak killing spree? Have you seen any of the shit that's out there? That's not a fucking killing spree, that's a fucking slaughter. A calculated, systematic, merciless slaughter." He paused, stepping back to put space between him and the rep. "This wasn't some guy with a gun, your entire fucking colony murdered each other, and then whoever was left, or thought they were left, finished themselves off." He paused, inhaling sharply as his gaze locked to Talmadge. "I know what you're trying to do;

plausible deniability, and it isn't gonna work. You assholes aren't gonna weasel your way out of this one. No, not while I still have breath. That option died with my corporal. No.

You're gonna burn for this."

Hawkes shifted, stepping slightly closer to Baker.

Baker lifted his gaze to the red landscape outside and then made his way around the desk to stand near Hawkes as he regrouped himself.

Talmadge held his tongue, fury burning inside him as he continued flipping through file after file, marking each one for deletion as he did.


Dom, Wilkes and Lanskey had returned to medical, the three of them removing the cloth wrapped around their face as the hallway door leading to the director's room shut behind them.

"How long until that smell goes away?" Dom asked, coughing into the shirt he'd used to block the odor.

Lanskey started directly towards the computer terminal, responding as she did. "Decomposition can take up to three months in perfect conditions. I'd say we're gonna be long gone from here before it does. It's actually gonna get worse as the gasses built up in the bodies begin to expel. All we're dealing with right now is the smell of coagulated blood, urine and feces expelled upon death, and the minor onset of rot. The worst is still to come."

"Remind me not to ask you any more questions like that," Dom replied with a shake of the head and disgusted look on his face.

"I would have assumed you would have been used to the smell by now," she added. "You've been near decomp before, right?"

"Yeah," Dom replied, taking a deep breath and exhaling slowly. "But not like this. Rwanda was different.

This is…" He let the sentence trail off.

"I guess we'll have to see what you can find Doc," Wilkes said. "The sooner we're done here the better. This place is creeping me out."

Lanskey sat down at the computer without a reply. She cracked her knuckles while exhaling deeply and then leaned forward, bringing the screen to life. Immediately she began sifting through case report after case report. She was determined to find something. There was always some small detail that got skipped over, something that slipped through the cracks upon initial investigation. She knew there had to be something there.

"Might as well get comfortable, Wilkes said, sliding a chair across the floor to Dom. "We're gonna be here for a while."

"Great…" Dom replied, turning to glance into the hall before making his way to the chair.

"Look," Baker said, stepping back from the desk. "Whatever it is that's in this station needs to be contained. I'm not trying to be difficult, but right now, we're as good as blind. And unless you wanna end up like the people in the hallways out there, then you need to start playing ball."

Talmadge slammed his hands on the desk, the sound erupting in the room. Hawkes turned, his rifle twitching at the outburst. Baker looked across the room and quickly shook his head. The Corporal lowered his weapon while still maintaining eye contact.

"I don't know any more than you do," Talmadge hissed, his palms still flat on the desk. "I arrived here at the same time as you, on the same ship. I walked into this station right behind you, so I've had enough of this conspiracy theory bullshit. I'm done. There is no evil plot by Xenocorp, no hidden treasure we're trying to keep, no alien species to bring back to Earth for testing, none of that shit. People are dead, every one of the colonists that came here are dead, entire families, dead. Do you think I don't know this? I've been walking through the same hallways as you. I'm not blind. Now forgive me if I, just as you, have a job to do here." He stiffened. "You have to protect your soldiers, and I, just like you, have to protect the trillion-dollar company I work for. If I don't do that, then when we get back to Earth, my job, my career, the only thing I have going for me, will be gone. And in that case, I may as well just join the rest of them in the hall, because I don't have anything else. Now I am tired of you treating me like I'm some kind of spy, trying to sabotage your mission. I'm just doing the same thing as you; trying to survive." He took a deep breath, pulling his hands from the desk. "Now, I've looked through every file on this computer, the same ones you have on that nanodrive, and there's nothing, nothing, about what it was they found out there. All we know, is that they broke into that damn pyramid, and shortly after, the entire colony went batshit and started offing each other. That's basically, exactly what I'm going to report when we get back. Now if we could be done with this whole pissing contest, I'd be really grateful, because to put it lightly, I am scared shitless right now, because I'm sitting in a space station millions of miles from Earth, surrounded by hundreds of dead bodies, and whatever the hell it was that did this, is still roaming around in here somewhere. I just want to get the hell out of here, and go back home so I can take my long overdue vacation, which I planned to go to the New Republic of France, and visit the remains of the Eiffel Tower."

The soldier had finally pushed him to the point of snapping. He kept his useless threats packed away, instead, filing them for use once they were back to Earth. He also knew that yelling never accomplished anything, that ninety-nine percent of the time, only served to exacerbate the situation, but he had had it. As long as the sergeant kept feeding into the other soldier's image of him being a slimy rat, then it was going to be even that much harder for him to complete his task. With the way things had turned out, he realized that he may even find himself needing their help to keep a tight lid on things, and at the same time, digging a paper grave for their sergeant. Bribing and blackmail were the least of his concerns, but he knew things would go that much smoother if the men didn't think he was the enemy. One thing he wouldn't accept, was some low grade military asshole thinking he could put him in his place. He had dedicated his entire life to the company that for all accounts and purposes, even allowed the military to take part in missions like this one. Hell, they had even funded, anonymously of course, the creation of the EMF, when the top ten governments of the world had decided it best to unify their militaries in order to keep a stronger control over the smaller rebel factions that had risen up after Rwanda and the wars that followed. He would not stand there and take orders from some min-pay asshole with a couple stripes glued to his shirt. He didn't on Earth, and he sure as shit wasn't going to here, in the facility that he had watched grow from paper concept to the installation they now stood in.

Baker stared at the rep for a moment, a thin smile growing across his lips. He glanced up to see Wilkes smirk with a nod of approval. "Well, okay," Baker replied, his smile growing. "Then why don't we go find this thing, kill it or contain it, and then get the hell off this rock."

Talmadge stood up, watching the sergeant make his way to the other soldier. The moment his back was to him he clicked delete and erased all the files containing information on the facility breakdown.

"Sarge," Vuong clicked across the comm. "I think I got something. How quickly can you get back here?"

"We're on our way," Baker replied, glancing to Wilkes before turning his gaze back to Talmadge. "Looks like Vuong might have something. What do you say we go find out what this thing is?"

Talmadge nodded, turning to make his way to where Wilkes stood. Together the three started back down the hall towards security, the palpable tension remaining in the room, a thick cloud left behind.

16

"Lanskey?"

The sergeant's voice cracked across the headset like lightning, startling the chief officer in her seat. She composed herself as his voice continued to crackle in her ear.

"Vuong thinks he might have found something. We're heading back to security to check it out. Anything new on your end?"

She pulled her gaze from the computer monitor and let it fall to a large stack of file folders on the desk near her. "I've got a lot of reports all starting around the same time. I'm sorting through them as quickly as possible, but it's going to take a while. I need to be thorough. I'll let you know the moment I find something."

"Copy that. Keep me posted."

She took a deep breath, glancing back to Wilkes and shaking her head. "Scared the shit out of me..."

Wilkes smiled, the sterile lights in the room emphasizing the discolored bags beginning to grow beneath his eyes. "Surprised you're not used to it yet." She shook her head again and turned back to the screen.

Dom grinned at Wilkes and then paused as a faint sound filtered past his ear. He turned his head to the hallway and listened for another few seconds. "You hear that?" he asked, shifting his rifle.

Wilkes turned his head towards the doorway for a moment, concern knitting his eyebrows together. "No." He listened for another moment before a cough from Lanskey pulled his attention back to the monitor in front of her, the pretty face of a young girl's admin photo keeping his attention there. "Didn't hear anything."

"I'm gonna check it out," Dom said, turning to make his way into the hallway.

Wilkes nodded, his eyes still locked to the pretty face of the hopeful youth, a hydroponics specialists from what the title beneath said. Pity she wasn't still alive, he could use the diversion.

Dom slipped into the hallway, every muscle taut, the silence pressing in on him like a physical weight. The corridor ahead curved sharply out of sight, its far end swallowed by shadow. He moved heel-to-toe, each step deliberate, his breath shallow, the only sound the faint scuff of his boots on the metal floor. He paused at the corner, heart hammering, and pressed his back to the wall, listening—nothing but the distant hum of the station's dying systems.

He forced himself to move, rifle raised to his chest, and swung around the corner in a single, fluid motion. The hallway was empty. The door at the far end was closed, the overhead lights flickering, casting the walls in a sickly, stuttering glow. For a moment, Dom let out a shaky breath, feeling foolish for his nerves. He almost laughed—almost—until the air shifted.

A sudden, unnatural cold swept over him, slicing through his suit and skin, burrowing into his bones. He froze. The temperature plummeted, breath fogging inside his helmet. Out of the corner of his eye, something moved—a shimmer, barely perceptible, like heat rising off asphalt, but wrong, inverted, a ripple of darkness that seemed to suck the light from the air.

Dread crashed over him, primal and absolute. His mind screamed at him to run, to drop to the floor and curl up, to do anything but stand there, exposed. But his body refused to obey. He was paralyzed, every muscle locked, as if invisible hands were holding him in place. The shadows seemed to pulse, reaching for him, whispering threats just beyond hearing.

Sweat broke out across his brow, stinging his eyes. His fingers curled involuntarily, nails biting into his palms, and his jaw clenched so hard he tasted blood. Panic clawed at his chest, his vision tunneling, heart pounding so loudly he thought it might burst. For a single, endless moment, he was certain something was behind him, breathing down his neck.

Then, as suddenly as it began, the sensation vanished. The cold receded. Dom staggered, gasping, his legs trembling. He stood there, shaking, the metallic taste of blood thick on his tongue where he'd bitten down. His head throbbed, pain lancing behind his eyes. He swallowed, throat raw, and forced himself to move, to put one foot in front of the other.

That's when he heard it—a faint, scraping sound from the room where Lanskey and Wilkes were working. It was thin, almost insectile, like claws on glass, but beneath it was something else: a wet, rattling breath, the sound of lungs half-rotted, thick with blood and decay. Every instinct screamed at him to run, but he forced himself forward, voice cracking as he called out, "Wilkes?" and hurried toward the room, pulse roaring in his ears.

"None of this makes sense," Lanskey said, glancing up for a second to Wilkes who stood huddled over her shoulder. "The only similarity I can find in these cases are the reports of phantom voices and the onset of headaches leading up to migraines." She stopped, flipping through three files quickly. Her eyes squinted together and she paused, holding her breath for a moment. Just as Wilkes was about to speak up she burst out softly. "Hold up... These reports are from the earliest reported cases, reports of patients hearing and seeing dead relatives, monsters, giant insects, a whole number of other things. What if, and bear with me, cause I know how crazy this sounds. What if, whatever is causing this, is using hallucinations to trigger the violence? What if... What if, somehow, it's using our fears, to create a reaction leading to murders and suicides that have occurred? What if the colonists weren't killing each other, but thought they were killing giant spiders or the boogeyman from their childhood? What if they had no idea they were killing each other?"

She turned to Wilkes who slowly brought his gaze to meet hers. What she was implying was that it was it a sentient being, and capable of eradicating an entire colony without even making physical contact.

"Shit..." Wilkes whispered, the weight of her words landing heavy in his ears.

Dom crept back toward the room, his pulse thundering in his ears. He paused at the threshold, breath caught in his throat. The lights flickered, casting warped shadows across the walls. For a split second, the scene before him seemed wrong—distorted, as if reality itself was bending.

Leaning over Lanskey was a figure—Wilkes, or something wearing his face. Its posture was all wrong, too rigid, too predatory. The eyes that glanced up at Dom were hollow, glinting with a malice that Wilkes had never possessed. For a heartbeat, Dom's mind refused to process what he was seeing: the fingers curled into unnatural claws, the skin stretched tight over shifting bone, the mouth twisted in a silent snarl.

A cold realization crashed over him. Whatever had been stalking them through the station had taken Wilkes—killed him, and now wore his form like a mask. The horror of it rooted Dom to the spot. He understood, in a flash of sick clarity, how the colony had fallen: the thing killed, then imitated, drawing closer to its next victim with every stolen face.

Lanskey, oblivious, continued typing at the console, her voice a distant murmur. Dom's hands trembled as he raised his rifle, sweat slicking his grip. The thing that looked like Wilkes turned, its gaze locking onto him, and for a moment, Dom saw something flicker beneath the surface—something ancient, hungry, and utterly inhuman.

"Dom?" it said, Wilkes' voice warped by something deeper, something wrong. "Put the rifle down."

Lanskey began to turn, confusion creasing her brow. Dom's finger tightened on the trigger, every instinct screaming at him to fire, to run, to do anything but stand there. As Lanskey's face came into view, Dom's breath caught. Her features were wrong—torn, twisted, one eye ruined and leaking, her mouth stretched into a grotesque, toothy grin that split her face in two.

Dom's world spun. The cold in the room deepened, pressing in on him from all sides. He realized, with a surge of terror, that he was alone— truly alone—with the monsters that had once been his friends.

"Dom, what are you doing?" Lanskey said as the soldiers dilated eyes set upon her. "Dom, it's me, it's Barbara. You know me. You know Terrance too. Please. Put the gun down, Dom."

Slowly Wilkes raised his arms and began to step forward, his hand moving to the comms button on his helmet.

Dom's finger squeezed the trigger, the rifle bucking against his shoulder as he unleashed a desperate barrage. The thunder of gunfire filled the medical bay, muzzle flashes strobing across the carnage. He didn't stop—couldn't stop—until the thing wearing Wilkes' face and the twisted mockery of Lanskey were nothing but a crumpled, twitching heap on the blood-slick floor.

The room was a ruin. Bullet holes riddled the walls, blood splattered in wild arcs across shattered equipment and broken tiles. The stench of cordite and copper hung thick in the air, burning his nostrils, mingling with the sickly sweet rot of death. Dom's scream echoed off the metal, raw and animal, as he emptied the magazine into the monsters that had once been his friends.

And then—silence. The cold that had wormed its way into his bones remained, a glacial numbness spreading through his veins, hollowing him out from the inside. He stared at the bodies, his mind reeling, unable to reconcile the faces on the floor with the memories of laughter and camaraderie that haunted him.

Hopelessness crashed over him, suffocating and absolute. There was no escape, no fighting back. The thing that had taken them—taken everyone—was unstoppable, inevitable. He could feel it now, coiling inside him, whispering in a voice colder than the Martian night.

Dom's hands trembled as he lowered the rifle, the weight of what he'd done pressing down on him like a physical force. Tears blurred his vision, streaking his cheeks as the horror of his actions settled in. He had killed them—his family, his unit, the only people he had left.

Slowly, mechanically, he raised the rifle to his chin, the barrel icy against his skin. His finger tightened on the trigger, and in the suffocating silence, a whisper slithered past his ear—soft, insidious, promising oblivion.

*"The others are coming."*

He pressed his eyes closed and drew back the pressure on the trigger. With his last grasp of control, he thought of the others. No. Somehow he had been used; manipulated to kill those he cared about, those he was supposed to protect. As his finger tightened he made the decision. No more of his friends would die because of him.

17

"Did you see that?" Vuong asked Sarge who was staring intently at the screen.

"Yeah," Baker replied. "The guy fired his weapon at the wall and then put the barrel in his mouth and pulled the trigger."

"No," Vuong said, his hand reaching out to rewind the footage on the monitor. "Not that." He brought his hand up and pointed at the monitor. "*That*." Baker leaned closer.

"Right there, before the guy shoots at the wall, something moved. Just watch. It's like a shadow, or a shimmer." He pressed play and leaned back, waiting for the moment before the man raised his pistol. "There, watch!"

Baker stared as the security feed in the room showed a colonist in mining apparel sitting at a desk with a pistol in his hand. He was staring blankly at the opposite wall, and then, at the edge of the screen, almost unnoticeable, something translucent moved past, a nearly invisible vapor, just enough to cause a ripple against the wall behind it. Then the man raised his pistol and fired three times at the space before turning the gun on himself.

"Can you slow that down?" Baker asked, rubbing his eyes before staring back at the screen. He could feel a nervous excitement ripple through him.

Vuong started the video again, slowing it to twenty-five percent the moment the shimmer occurred. Then Baker saw the almost non-existent movement.

A grim realization crept through him, a nervousness bordering on fear slowly penetrating. *No way... No...*

"Jesus Christ," he whispered, his eyes still locked to the screen. "It's fucking camouflaged."

"Well, that would explain why nobody saw anything. 'Cause there's nothing to see. Whatever the hell that thing is, it's fucking invisible."

"Goddamnit," Baker hissed. "Mills, get Lanskey on the horn and tell her we found what the hell it is that killed everyone and why we couldn't find it. You tell them to get their asses back here on the double."

"Roger," Mills snapped, moving to step out of the room.

Baker shifted his gaze to Vuong. "My next question is, how do we kill it?"

Vuong pulled up the facility schematics. The facility unfolded before them in a series of white lines across a blue screen. Every tunnel, every duct and ventilation shaft was laid out before them. The group stared at the screen for a moment before Vuong continued. "We have multiple entry points," he began. "We can seal off everything we don't need access to, like the sci-labs, hydroponics, administration, the central core. That way, at least if it can't travel through walls, it'll either be trapped in one of those sections, or forced to come to us. We could funnel it somehow."

"Yeah," Baker replied. "But that's if the thing can't travel through walls... We don't even know what this thing is, or what it's made of. We don't know shit." He paused, his gaze moving to Vuong who sat looking up at him. "There must have been a reason someone built that thing out there, buried it and kept it hidden this whole time. Must have been a pretty important reason too..." His thoughts wandered to the dead colonists that filled the facility around them.

"Fire's pretty universal," Fascio said after a moment.
"We could burn the fucker."

"Okay." Baker replied, pulling himself from the vapors of hopelessness that had begun to envelope him. "That's one idea."

"All we need to do is contain it," Hawkes said, stepping forward. "As long as it can't get loose, we can get off planet and wait for a clean-up crew to come take care of the rest. If it could move through walls, then the door in the vid wouldn't have opened, it would have just come right through."

Baker turned to the youngest of the unit and clenched his teeth together. "You have a point there, but don't think for a moment we're going to just turn tail and run. That's one thing we won't be doing." He paused, his gaze hard and unforgiving. "That thing killed Corlin, and we aren't leaving until we show it what happens when you kill one of ours."

"I wasn't suggesting—"

"That's exactly the point," Baker barked, the piercing behind his eyes flaring up. "You weren't suggesting anything. And you're gonna keep it that way." He turned back to Fascio. "So where do we get fire?"

"Sarge," Mills said, stepping back into the room. "I'm not getting any response. I tried all three of them. Nothing."

Hollow dread slowly crept into the room.

"You gotta be shitting me," Baker growled.

"Lanskey, Wilkes?" he shouted across the comm. "DiLeonardo. Come in, over!" There was no reply, only the sound of the circulation fans overhead. "Lanskey, respond goddamnit!"

"Sarge...?"

Baker looked at Vuong and then exhaled sharply.

"Med lab. Now!"

18

The group made their way through housing. The moist chill that still hung in the air around them continued to press inwards, the noxious vapors of death filtering past their noses. None of them spoke, their minds working the events unfolding around them. A grease-covered knot continued to build in the sergeant's stomach, growing tighter as they approached medical.

Baker stopped at the door, holding up his hand and turning his head to shoot Fascio a concerned look before gesturing for him to take point. The other nodded, shifting his rifle to the back and unslinging his newly acquired shotgun. He took a deep breath, exhaling heavily in front of him and then started down the hall. With every step he half-expected the corpses contained in the bags along the floor to jump up and attack them. He made the extra motion to give the canvas bags as wide of a berth as possible. The lights had begun to flicker again and he could hear something creaking deeper in the facility, the steel bones flexing as the heat allowed the sleeping giant to stretch. The team continued inwards, and when they reached the section of the corridor that angled out of view, they instinctively slowed before turning the edge. When they did, the lights overhead flickered again, strobing the hallway in pulses that strained their eyes to see ahead of them. The facility continued to mock their movements, making every effort to stifle their advance. Unknown to them, the monster hidden in the darkness waited patiently. Time not measured in human terms had passed in its existence, the minutes it took the men to make their way there was nothing, a blink in existence unnoticed.

"I hate this fucking place," Mills whispered, swallowing hard as he squinted tightly against the flashing illumination.

Fascio stepped around the curve and stopped. His eyes locked to a puddle of dark liquid slowly seeping from beyond the doorway of the director's office. He turned to look at Sarge who tensed, moving his rifle to his shoulder before stepping in front and approaching the doorway. As he neared it he realized what the liquid was, and that the way it was moving, it had just been spilled.

The creature the humans hunted hung invisibly on the ceiling, a vapor clinging to steel as it watched the men approach. Slowly it pressed itself flat. It would wait. It was patient, and time was nothing but an unknown sensation to it. It had already had its fill for the time being. The newest arrivals were simply an addition.

Baker's heart began to beat heavily in his chest, a thin line of sweat working its way across his forehead as he stepped closer. He was less than ten feet away when a voice, like a memory, phantom in the room, whispered past his ear.

*"They did this."*

Baker stopped, the flesh across his back tightening against his solid frame. He glanced behind him to the fear glazed eyes of his unit. *It's just the station*, he told himself as he turned back to the doorway looming darkly ahead. *This place is fucking with me*. He stepped closer to the room, dim emergency lights slowly flickering to life as another thin groan of constricted steel cried out overhead.

Before he breached the room he stopped, turning to his men one last time. He knew that no matter what, they would have his back, but there was something pulling him backwards, begging him not to enter. He could feel the still air in the hallway stagnant around him and smelled the all-too-familiar mixture of blood and gunpowder wafting from within. Before he even stepped forward he knew what lay in wait.

The light from Baker's gun sliced through the darkness as he spun into the room, the beam trembling in his grip. The scene that met him was a tableau of horror. Dom lay sprawled on his side just feet away, his helmet shattered, the upper half of his skull gone— brain and bone scattered in grotesque fragments across the floor. Wilkes was crumpled near the desk, his body riddled with bullet wounds, face nearly unrecognizable save for the blood-soaked strip of canvas bearing his name.

Lanskey slumped in a chair, her torso riddled with holes, dead eyes staring glassy and unblinking at a patch of floor near Baker's boots. The air was thick with the stench of blood and gunpowder, copper and iron mingling with the acrid tang of spent rounds. Death pressed in from every corner, suffocating and absolute.

Baker stood frozen, his mind a storm of panic and disbelief. Instinct screamed at him to run, to flee the carnage, but his training held him rooted, forcing him to take in every detail. His gaze darted from one fallen comrade to the next—men and women who, less than an hour ago, had been alive, laughing, fighting beside him. Now they were nothing but ruined flesh, their stories ended in violence and terror.

He felt his grip tighten on the rifle, knuckles white, as a wave of helpless rage threatened to break through his composure. The urge to scream, to curse the thing that had done this, rose in his throat, but he swallowed it down, jaw clenched so hard it ached. All he could do was stare, the silence of the room broken only by the pounding of his own heart and the distant, mocking echo of lives lost forever.

"What the fuck!?" Fascio blurted from behind him, snapping him from the red haze that hung in front of his eyes. "Oh shit. No no no. This isn't fuckin' happening..."

Chaos wormed its way through the group, an icy blanket that slipped between them, into them. Behind them, a thin vapor wisped across the ceiling, disappearing out of view.

The others moved into the room, stopping as their eyes fell on the scene before them.

"No way," Mills whispered. "There's no way. We just spoke to them. This can't be…"

The unit's voices faded to the background as Baker stared at the carnage, his true instincts quickly lurching forward. "This just happened," he whispered as the others continued to panic behind him.

"We've gotta get out of here man!" Mills shouted above the others. "It's gonna fucking kill us! We gotta go."

"Shut up!" Baker yelled, turning around to grab Mills by the vest and slamming him against the wall next to the doorway. "You pull your shit together marine, and you do it now, or I'm gonna pull it together for you. Do you fucking copy!?"

Mills stared at the sergeant, eyes wild, a gazelle trapped in a lion's grasp. Slowly he nodded, his gaze not moving from the man who held him a half inch off the floor.

"Good," Baker growled, setting the man down and turning to look over the scene again. "As I was saying. This just happened. Look." He pointed to the blood and tissue hanging from the ceiling, and held his finger out until a drop formed and fell to the floor below. He moved to where Dom lay and knelt down, hovering his hand just over the barrel of the rifle. "His gun is still warm." Slowly he stood, turning to the others, his words lowering to a whisper. "Whatever did this, it's still here."

The others shifted nervously, their gazes moving to every dark space in the room.

Every corner had eyes, every shadow jagged talons.

Baker took a deep breath. He knew the impact of what he was about to say, but also knew, at this moment, things had gotten well out of control. The situation was no longer in their hands. "Let's move. I'm not gonna let any more of us die for a paycheck, especially one signed by the assholes that caused this in the first place. Fuck this station. We're getting the hell out of here."

"Sarge?" Vuong asked, pulling the sergeant's gaze to him. "What about them?"

Baker turned his gaze to their dead friends, finally stopping to rest on Dom.

"We can't leave them here."

Baker stared at the crumpled body at his feet. What seemed like an eternity passed before he was able to form his words. "We. We can't run the risk of bringing an unknown pathogen, or virus back with us." He paused, his words stabbing into him, a lie wrapped in fear. "Let's just get out of here, and once the cleanup crew arrives, we'll come back for them." He tried to convince himself that the words he spoke were true, but he knew the moment they got free of the planet's atmosphere, he would immediately put them on course back to Earth. He wasn't going to sit in orbit waiting for another unit to arrive. He'd lost four men on this mission, and wasn't going to wait around so that he could see more marines lost. They were done. They had survived, and now, they got to go home. There was nothing more they could do. They were simply not outfitted for this type of situation, and didn't have the weapons or manpower to engage. Nor did they even understand the enemy if they were to. "Sarge, do you read me? It's

Portofino, over."

Talmadge stood silently behind them, a ripple of fear and excitement working its way beneath his shirt.

Baker brought his hand up to the comms on his helmet and clicked over. "I read you. What's the status, over?"

"I heard knocking at the rear hatch. Are you still inside the facility? Over."

"That is affirmative, Corporal. Do not open that hatch, I repeat, you are not, under any circumstance, are you to open that hatch. You keep that ship secure until you see me standing in front of it, do you understand?"

The interior lights of the ship's control panel illuminated the pilot's features as she stared at the view screen in front of her, the empty tarmac in full view. She was positive she had heard knocking. When she clicked the sergeant, his response came back as a thin series of garbled words layered in static.

"Affirmative...*shhhhik*, Open the hatch.... *ssshhhhk*"

"Well, you could have at least given me a head's-up," she smirked, standing up to make her way to the back of the ship. She stopped at the exit hatch and engaged her envirosuit, sealing it before reaching up to engage the outer hatch. As the door opened, the air inside vented out in a loud cloud that dissipated as the planet's atmosphere dissolved it instantly. She looked up and shook her head, exhaling with a click of her tongue as the frigid air moved through her into the ship.

"Portofino?" Sarge barked into the comm. "Do you read me?"

The comms went silent, not even static replying.

Baker felt a solid lump building deep within his gut, a gross amalgamation of bile and fear slowly growing larger. Somehow, whatever had done this, had immediately gone to cut off their retreat. Whatever it was they were dealing with seemed to know their next move. Whatever it was they were now up against, was intelligent, and tactical. It knew they were going to go to the ship and try to make their way off the surface, and it was making sure that didn't' happen.

"Portofino!?" he shouted one last time before glancing to Fascio in the doorway. "Shit! Everybody get to the ship, now!"

The men turned and started their way quickly down the hall. As they dashed past the admissions office, Portofino's voice clicked back on.

"Where's everyone else, Sarge?"

Baker skidded to a stop, the others halting in front of them as they turned. Portofino's words stabbed through the headset.

"Portofino, we're still in the facility, do you copy?"
"What? How..?"
"Portofino, I repeat, I am still inside Attis. Who are you speaking to? Respond!" A familiar chill worked through him.

"But. If I blow the ship, then how do we get home? I need to get to my daughter. I need to see her again..." There was sadness in the pilot's voice, a distant anguish that trembled her words.

"Portofino! Fuck!" Baker had already started running before he yelled to the others. "MOVE!"

The unit rushed through the hallway. The sound of their boots clanking heavy echoed through the silent corridors as they pounded across the titanium floor, the flickering lights and sparking conduits flying past them as they raced towards the entrance. They were minutes away, but already Baker felt the sense of dread crescendoing behind his heartbeat that continued to grow as they bolted down the end of the hallway to the inner hatch. *How the fuck had that thing made it to the ship so quickly?*

As Mills ran behind he could hear the voices in his ears telling him to stop, to rest. He was tired, and there was no need to run, the ship would still be there. The whispers kept pace with him, soft voices gently lulling him slower in pace. He didn't need to stay with the rest, he could meet them there. Everything was going to be fine. He pounded one balled fist against the side of his head and continued forward, picking his pace back up with the others.

Baker reached the inner hatch and immediately began suiting up, pulling the sleeves to the envirosuit on frantically. The others stopped behind him, setting their rifles down as they did the same. A moment later he was suited up and turned to the others who were nearly done.

"Mills!" Baker yelled, seeing the youngest of them standing behind the others, staring at the floor with a dazed look in his eyes.

Mills looked up at him blankly, staring for a moment before nodding and setting his rifle down.

"Any day now, soldier," Baker yelled, waiting for the other to finish engaging his suit.

The moment Mills' suit sealed he turned and engaged the inner hatch, moving in as quickly as possible. "Portofino? We're at the outer hatch of the facility, do you copy, over?"

The door sealed behind them, the atmosphere venting out as the outer air filled the space. Then Baker engaged the second door.

As they exited the airlock, the ship loomed in the distance, exactly where they'd left it—fifty meters away, its hull stark against the barren Martian landscape. Baker broke into a run, urgency pounding in his veins, but stopped short as Portofino emerged from behind the vessel, her movements tense and deliberate.

She had just finished rigging the explosive charge to the fuel cells, her hands trembling as she secured the final connection. Salted lines of tears streaked down her face inside the helmet, the memories of her fallen unit flashing before her eyes. Sarge's words echoed in her mind—every one of them dead, hunted by something that wore their faces and stalked the corridors with silent malice.

Portofino's breath fogged the visor as she scanned the horizon, knowing what she had to do. The monsters in the facility would try to escape, would try to use the ship to reach Earth. If even one of them made it back, humanity itself would be lost. She would not allow that. Not after everything she'd seen. Not after the horrors that had claimed her friends.

As she stepped around the back of the ship, the dread became suffocating. She saw the twisted remains of the crew, the evidence of violence and betrayal, and knew the nightmare was not over. The monsters were close—closer than ever—and she was the last line of defense between them and the world beyond.

"Portofino!" Baker yelled as the pilot made her way from behind the ship.

The pilot stopped, her gaze turning terrified as she stared at them. Then she turned and darted inside the open hatch.

"NO!"

Baker flinched as a shape moved past him, a frantic blur that was Hawkes.

"I can't stay here!!!!"

"Shit!" Baker shouted, moving forward in an instant.

Before Baker's foot could touch the titanium deck, a violent blast erupted, hurling him backwards in a storm of heat and debris. The sky above ignited as the ship's fuel cells detonated, a roaring plume of fire swallowing the landing pad before vanishing almost instantly into the thin, alien atmosphere. For a heartbeat, the world was nothing but chaos—sound and fury, metal and flame.

He slammed into the outer hatch of the facility, the impact rattling his bones, ears ringing with the deafening aftermath of the explosion. Stunned, he lay sprawled on his side, vision swimming as he stared up at the fading column of smoke. Where TS-163 had stood, only a twisted heap of scorched titanium and warped steel remained—their only way home, reduced to wreckage.

Shock gripped him, breaths coming in short, ragged bursts. The ringing in his helmet drowned out every other sound, leaving him isolated in a cocoon of panic and disbelief. Slowly, he forced himself upright, hands trembling as he took in the devastation. Fascio and Vuong had drawn close, their faces pale, arms limp at their sides, rifles dangling uselessly.

"Sergeant," Talmadge's voice crackled through the comms, snapping Baker's attention away from the ruined ship. He turned to see Talmadge kneeling beside Mills, who was slumped against a metal crate, blood pooling beneath him. A jagged shard of metal protruded from Mills' suit, the nano-fabric sealed tight around the wound but failing to stop the relentless flow.

"We need to get him to medical," Vuong said urgently, inspecting the injury. The steel had punctured Mills' chest, crushing one lung and flooding the other with blood. Mills gasped for air, each breath a desperate, wet struggle. Baker pressed his fingers to his temples, fighting to focus as Vuong's voice cut through the haze. "Sarge! We need to get him to medical!"

Baker knelt beside Mills, searching the young marine's eyes for any sign of hope. Mills whispered something, voice barely audible, then slumped sideways, pupils dilating beneath the cracked visor. He took two more shuddering, liquid-filled gulps of air before his chest stilled, the silence settling heavy and final. "He's gone," he whispered, his eyes still affixed to the dead man's gaze.

"What are we gonna do?" Fascio asked, rising to his feet and turning to the burnt ship. "That was our only way off this rock..."

Silence hung between the group, the crimson and orange surface reflecting across their faces, casting a sickly tone to their skin.

"Not necessarily," Talmadge said, his voice barely heard through the comms.

"What are you talking about?" Baker hissed, turning his gaze to the rep who stared down at the dead soldier.

"There's an emergency ship. It's held here specifically for Xenocorp personnel, in case of an emergency evacuation or, unforeseen disaster." He paused, his gaze moving from the dead soldier to the sergeant whose eyes bored into him. "It's in the cargo bay at the other end of the facility."

Baker stared at him for a moment before speaking. "Well, I'd say this is pretty fucking unforeseen to me. Fascio, Vuong, we're moving out. Talmadge, why don't you just go ahead and show us where that ship is."

The others stood reluctantly, tradition and morals holding them to their dead friend's side. Everything that was happening around them was indescribable, but the feeling even worse than that, was leaving their brothers lying where they died and simply walking away. They both knew the response if they asked, and simply exchanged a glance that shared their pain.

"This is fucked," Fascio whispered as he made his way back to the hatch.

19

The air vented back into the room with a loud gush. As soon as the inner hatch was opened, they removed their envirosuits and started their way back into the derelict facility. The smell of death hung in a putrid cloud all around them and the floor had gone from slippery to a light tackiness that clung to their boots as they stepped down the hall. As they made their way down the empty corridors they could feel the invisible eyes of the station piercing through them, blood-splattered walls stalking them as they passed. Thoughts were kept to themselves, no words shared as they silently traversed the lonely corridors. The events that had unfolded and everything leading up to it smothered their words in their throats. All that was left was getting to the emergency ship, and making it off-planet before whatever had murdered their friends managed to take them out as well. They found themselves having quickly transitioned from hunter to prey, and whatever it was that was now beginning to pick them off was growing ever hungrier with each kill. Time was running thin and a quiet desperation worked through their steps.

They passed admissions when Fascio's gaze fell upon two men who had been beaten to death. His eyes stayed glued to their corpses as he stepped past when the emotion that he had held stifled deep in his chest, one that was beginning to smother him, burst free. "We're gonna die here," he said, the subconscious thought crackling across the comms.

"You stow that shit, Marine," Baker growled, his gaze locked to the empty air in the hallway. "Ain't nobody gonna die. We're gonna get to that ship, get into orbit and let someone else come put out this smoldering shitstorm." He struggled to allow his words to convince him as they fell out. Even he was beginning to struggle.

Fascio hadn't realized he had spoken out loud.

"Hawkes just had a baby girl last month," Vuong said, the image of the soldier exploding in front of him flashing past his eyes.

Baker stopped, turning to look at the three men. "We all have somebody we want to get home to. But we also have an entire planet of people that are depending on us holding it together here. Remember, whatever the fuck it is that's doing this... if it gets off this planet, there's gonna be a lot of newborn babies without fathers. There's gonna be a lot of fathers without their newborns, because the whole planet's gonna end up just like this colony. So, for the last time, pull your shit together."

Vuong stared at him for a moment, staring deeply into the two swirling black portals ringed by a thin strip of deep brown. Then he rubbed his nose with a sniffle and nodded. "Aye, Sarge."

"Good," Baker continued, shooting Fascio an irritated glance. "Now, if you could do us a favor, and pull up the station schematics again and find us the quickest route to the cargo bay, I would very much appreciate it."

Vuong felt a deep loss wrapped around him like a cold suit of iron. Desperation smothered him and his stomach worked in a series of twisted knots as he pulled up his holowrist and projected a blueprint schematic of the facility in front of them. He couldn't get the faces of his friends and fellow marines out of his head. He could hear their laughs, and their jokes, he could almost feel them still standing in the hallway with him. There was a moment where he had to fight the urge to click them on the comms. It was surreal. Unreal. Fear and unease coated him in a waxy layer of hot perspiration, wrapping him tightly as he moved his arm up.

"It's there," Talmadge said, pointing his finger into the thin strips of blue and white. "Aft section of cargo, single hold. It's a one of the newer model transport vessels, capable of holding up to twenty-five comfortably and reaching safe distance in less than three minutes." He paused, catching himself pitching the company product again, a habit perfected over the years. "We just need to get there. I have the door code."

"And what do we do if that thing finds us first?" Fascio asked, pulling the man's attention to him.

"Vuong," Baker asked, turning his attention away from the rep. "Did you finish sealing off the unused areas in the facility?"

194

"Sorry, Sarge, everything started happening. I didn't have the chance. We're still wide open."

Baker nodded, glancing to Fascio for a moment.

"Then we're gonna get back to security, and finish that. Then we get through this station as quickly as possible, and we get the hell out of here."

"Yes sir," Vuong said, a small portion of reserve building back up at the thought. "Linear and smooth, no surprises."

"That's what I wanna hear, now let's get a move on. We're not getting paid by the hour."

The group continued their way further in, passing the corporate offices and turning into the housing and security hallway. As they passed environmental a thin whisper wafted past Baker's ear. *"Come home."*

He stopped, his gaze whipping to the sealed door. *That's not possible. It's the station. You're not real.* The voice behind the door smiled. *"Take us home daddy, take us home with you."*

"Everything okay, Sarge?" Vuong asked, turning to see the sergeant staring at the sealed door to environmental. The look on his face was equal parts fear and recognition. He could see where the lack of sleep was starting to build in dark rings under his eyes, and the shadows cast in the hallway eluded to his true age. An air of confusion filtered past his features for a moment and then he blinked heavily and turned his gaze to him.

"Sarge?"

Baker tore his gaze from the doorway, his eyes locking to his men. "Yeah. Just, double checking the seal. Wouldn't want enviro going out as we're making our way out."

Above them, silent on the ceiling a formless shimmer watched their every movement from the dark, studying its potential hosts as a thin ripple of excitement ebbed through it. Slowly it tested their strengths, their compatibility. It needed them weak. It needed them desperate and on the verge of collapse. By the time more arrived it would be ready for the journey to whatever system these creatures were from. Then the true feast would begin. Then...

Vuong nodded, his gaze still held to the sergeant.

Baker stepped past him, taking point and moving further down the hallway to the security room. As Vuong approached he tapped Fascio on the arm and nodded, his brow scrunched together as he did. "You catch that?" he whispered.

Fascio nodded, glancing to the door Sarge had just disappeared into. "Yeah."

Vuong nodded silently, moving to make his way into security. He'd caught it alright. Sarge had been looking at something. Something had caught his attention, and whatever it was, he was hiding it from them.

"So, I've sealed off every possible section we don't have to go through. As far as lockdown goes, we're as secure as we're gonna get. It's one straight shot from here to mining, and from there, past hydroponics to the cargo bay. If everything goes smoothly, we can be there in twenty minutes and off this station within the hour."

"Good," Baker replied, staring at the red lines across the screen.

A loud groan warped through the facility, steel grinding against steel as the structure's frame flexed. The building heat inside pressing against the frozen environment beyond bent the beams around them, stressing them, pressure building up as the temperature continued to slowly rise.

"It would be a lot quicker just to go past the sci-labs straight to cargo," Talmadge said, pointing to the monitor.

"Someone blew the entrance," Vuong says, clicking his fingers across the keys to pull up a surveillance image of the hallway.

A pile of rubble and twisted metal crates were piled in the doorway to the science labs. The doors had been blown inwards, with the walls surrounding them completely scorched. He panned the camera to the other doorway to cargo and showed them why that route wouldn't work. The explosion had cast debris to the other side of the hall, and collapsed the ceiling around the entrance to cargo.

"No way we're getting through that," Vuong said. "We gotta go around."

"Okay," Baker replied, bringing his hand up to the pulsing that pounded behind his right temple. "Then what are we still standing here for?"

20

Central housing stood empty, the vacant silence mocking their loss as they made their way past the tables they had broken bread together at that morning. A claustrophobic stillness stalked them, the whisper of groaning steel creeping just behind. As they passed through, Vuong could hear Corlin making wisecrack comments and Mills taking usual offense, phantom traces of their voices hanging on stagnant air. Fascio glanced in one of the rooms and saw the little boy standing near the wall at the back, face bloated and grey, wet hair dripping down his face to the shoulders of his striped shirt. He realized he had closed the door prior, and the fact that it now stood open, almost inviting, dug into him, images of faceless monsters and hidden horrors leaping to the surface. "We need to get out of here," he said, increasing his pace to get quickly out of reach of whatever it was that lay just inside.

"I couldn't agree more," Vuong replied, pushing the sounds from his ears. "You starting to see things too?" "Yeah," Fascio replied, his tone just quiet enough to evade the sergeant's ears. "It's time to go."

The creature was getting stronger, each death feeding its strength, giving it more energy in which to expend against the delicate minds of the fragile beings it stalked.

They made their way into the hallway, turning to go past medical where rows of black bags and fresh memories of the three dead marines at the end clawed at them. They continued past quietly, the corridor running a hundred feet before turning sharply to the right. Baker realized his gaze was locked to the floor as he walked, subconsciously avoiding lifting it in fear he would see his wife and daughter standing burnt and broken. He could hear them whispering just behind him, following just out of view, their presence reaching out to touch him with every step. Their presence had become increasingly stronger since they had left the pyramid, persisting to the point of him even getting wafts of perfume mixed with burnt rubber and oil. He struggled to press them back, repeating like a mantra that it was all in his head, that the facility was making it seem real, but he could feel the reality of it slowly slipping away as he whispered his responses silently under his breath, conscious not to let the others hear. They wouldn't understand. This facility had allowed him a way to bring them back, a means of being with them again. This station was becoming the key to him having a family again.

As they entered the next hall, the walls became bare, save for a single handprint that had been slapped against it. There was no blood, no rotting corpses, no scenes of carnage or coppery stench hanging in the air, just tan walls with recessed lighting shining clearly around them. Their steps echoed lightly as they made their way further, pausing before they continued past the corner into the end of the hall. There, at the end, thirty feet away, everything they had prepared themselves to encounter in the pristine hall, waited for them, a visceral mass at the end of the corridor.

The four of them paused, slowing as the sight before them registered. Just outside the door to mining was a jumble of tattered clothing and flesh, a matted patchwork of colonists, gunned down as they piled into each other against the sealed door. Whatever it was that they were trying to escape, cornered them at the end of the hall, and unloaded every round of ammunition it carried into them.

Vuong stepped forward, his feet sending dozens of spent casings across the floor, the light tinkling bringing a ripple to his skin. The group had been massacred, some of them lying shot at the top of the pile as they apparently tried to scramble over others to escape, but the locked door hadn't allowed them to. There were twenty colonists sprawled outwards from the barred door, a fetid knotwork of black and purple arms and legs now moist and covered in a thin layer of slime as the environment continued to level out.

"We need to—" Vuong started, pulling his gaze away as the urge to vomit rose in his throat.

"I'll give you a hand," Fascio said, staring at the mountain of corpses that blocked their way forward.

"Let's just get it done so we can get the hell out of here."

"Just give me a second," Vuong replied, kneeling over to take a deep breath before rising straight and turning to make his way towards it. He could feel the bile rising as he stepped closer, and his skin began to crawl as his fingers clasped around the first ankle. He forced his thoughts to wander, focusing on anything but the carnage before him. He thought about his youth, his family, the ride to the air base where they had launched from. He rerouted electronic components in his mind, recalculating for different load specifications. He and Fascio worked silently, hauling the corpses one by one away from the door until the area was clear enough for him to access the panel.

Baker stood silently next to Talmadge as his men cleared the dead, one by one, carrying them into the hallway so they could make their way past. When they finished, Vuong approached the door and pulled the cover from the keypad, exposing the wires. He ran the bypass cable from his holowrist to the panel and typed a series of numbers in. The light on the door switch clicked from red to green, signaling their path was open. "We're in," he said, pressing the door switch and stepping back quickly.

The door to mining opened with a groan. The lights inside were off, and the massive space cracked with soft metallic creaks, the sound of the door scraping against the floor echoing loudly an audible glimpse at the enormity of the space they were entering.

Fascio clicked his headlamp on and stepped inside, the flashlight on his rifle coming to light and illuminating the mining bay. Vuong followed immediately behind him, stepping in quickly, his tactical light flashing from one dark corner to another. Both men were scared, a fear surpassing their hairiest firefights drilling deeply within them. Neither of them spoke it, but they could each tell without asking by how shaky the beams of illumination skipped across the surfaces.

The bay was massive, nearly two hundred feet long and over fifty feet across, with a ceiling nearly as tall. Towering shelves made from corrugated metal ran horizontally along the walls, countless pieces of mining equipment lying still atop. Drills and hammers and pieces of electronic equipment used for seismic scanning lay covered in a thin layer of dust. The smell of metal shavings and oil hung heavy in the air. As they made their way in, a thin vibrating sound worked its way into their ears, almost unnoticeable at first, but persisting as they stepped further in.

"You hear that?" Fascio whispered as he scanned the room in front of them with his light.

"Ventilation," Vuong said, stepping in behind him.

Above them an invisible shape shifted silently, blackness rippling in a darkened corner, a stalking haze that had followed them unseen from the outer hatch to the ceiling of the bay they now stood in. Slowly it watched, eyeless and patient, observing the creatures below with a blank fascination, with delicate control it allowed its hunger to build again. Eons had passed since it was locked away, transported across countless galaxies and imprisoned in the retched space, confined by ancient markings; spells cast by beings sentient and long passed. The hunger it felt could never be quelled, and though its supply was waning thin, it was still weak. It had to be careful. It had to be patient. Those feelings pulsed through it again and again.

The pair started forward, shadows creeping all around them as their light bounced off the metallic surfaces. Every twenty feet, thick yellow and black lines crisscrossed the floor, marking designated holding stations. They could see where three large sections stood empty, the word Rover painted in block lettering inside the rectangular markers. The smell of steel and oil pressed into their nostrils even deeper and a thick layer of orange dust filled in the lines gouged into the steel deck beneath their feet.

Vuong glanced to a massive doorway on the opposite side of the room. Piled in front of the airlock were two of the rovers, a staggering jumble of steel beams and drilling rods jammed at sharp angles throughout, blocking off any escape through the doorway. He flashed his light through the twisted heap and saw that someone had taken the extra measure to weld a thick piece of titanium over the door hatch. The metal beneath showed black scarring where whoever had done it had destroyed the panel before covering it in extra measure. The mining bay had served as a last stand in a paranoid effort to keep the monsters at bay. A thin haze hung in the air, dust and sediment particles dancing lazily in front of his light. For the briefest of moments, he found himself thinking that if his situation were any different, he might have almost found a beauty in it, a serenity. He enjoyed the smell of mechanics, oil and scrap, and the tinge of welding smoke. But at that moment, it was an unnoticed thought as he wondered what the colonists must have seen to make them go to those measures of blocking the exit.

They continued forward, passing the blocked off passage and into a section lined with shelves on thin rails. The shelves were designed to close together against the walls in order to move the rovers in and out, but someone had jammed steel rods into the slots they moved along, locking them in place so none of the rovers could have made it through. Just beyond the shelves they came across four men lying next to each other, each ripped into with the industrial drill that lay cast aside nearby, the assailant long gone, a corpse undoubtedly rotting in a different section of the facility.

Baker stepped past, the darkness pulling heavily at him from all sides. He could see the sunken faces of the dead, hollowed eyes staring back at him from the floor. He could hear the almost unending whisper, an uninvited tenant taking residence in his mind. *"They are going to try and keep you here. They don't want us to leave."* He paused, his gaze locked to the corpses as his wife's words filtered unheard by others to his ears. *They would never let them leave. They wouldn't understand. They'd think he was crazy.*

Vuong glanced behind him at Fascio and Talmadge, and saw Sarge standing next to the dead men, his gaze staring down, eyebrows furrowed in what was a perfect blend of concern and bland confusion.

"Sarge?" he whispered, the sound of his voice echoing across the endless metal surfaces startling himself in the process. "Sarge!"

Baker turned his head. The three men were staring at him. He hadn't realized he'd zoned out.

"You all right, Sarge?" Vuong asked, a cracking sound snapping his gaze to the darkness to his side.

"Yeah," Baker replied, a soft anger slowly building inside him that the others thought something was wrong with him, that he was tainted. He knew they were conspiring to keep him from getting back to Earth. He had once trusted these men, known them. Talmadge was a piece of shit, and to be honest, he wished he could leave him there in the first place, but Vuong, Fascio. He had served with these men, fought on the battlefield with them, shared a barracks with them, his life. He felt a deep stabbing pain as their judgmental gazes held his. He felt resentment, and anger.

The creature above shifted, a translucent ripple against the black ceiling.

Vuong glanced to Fascio quickly as the sergeant glanced back to the dead men once more. "Okay, Sarge," he replied, trying his best not to look suspicious. "We're almost to that ship, then we can get the hell out of here and enjoy some of those mai tai's we talked about."

Baker stared at the corpses for another moment and then turned back to the men. "How much farther?" Vuong stared at him for a moment before replying. "Not far. Down the corridor past hydroponics. Hundred and fifty meters, tops." Something dug into him. The sergeant was vacant, disassociated and distant. Something about his demeanor felt... Off. The Sarge he knew was not the one he was speaking with, and that scared him.

"All right," Baker replied, his building hatred of the situation rising inside of him through the haze. "Then we keep moving, and if we're lucky, we'll come across that son of a bitch on our way there. It'll save us having to go looking for it..." He paused, his gaze moving back to the three men waiting ten feet away. "If we do, we show that thing what the EMF was created for." He could feel the rage burning. He'd lost his entire team, the unit he had been charged with was dead, the men he had overseen, murdered, killed by the monsters that still roamed the facility. He needed to get his family home, but that meant taking care of any threats in the way before he did.

"Sarge," Vuong said, confusion working through his words. "I thought we were gonna get to the ship and go?"

"Do you have a problem with following my orders, Marine?"

Fascio felt a ripple run across his skin. He felt it too, and as slowly as possible, shifted the shotgun strapped to his back a little closer to the front.

"No, Sir, not at all," Vuong replied. "I was just a little unclear on what our objective is."

The sergeant stared at him for a moment and then took a deep breath, exhaling sharply into the thick air. "Our objective is to get the hell off this rock, and back to Earth. If we happen to come across any threat in the process of doing so, we engage, and eradicate said threat." He paused, his gaze moving between Vuong and Fascio. "I thought I was pretty clear on that."

"Just wanted to double check, Sarge," Vuong replied, a thin layer of sweat building on his palms. "A lot's going on, and this place is starting to crawl under my skin."

"That thing, whatever it is, killed the rest of your unit. Your brothers, my men, they're all dead now. I want to kill it just as badly as you do, but if we make it out of here, and that thing hitches a ride back... We can't let that happen, so again, if we come across it between here and the ship.

Then we're gonna kill the hell out of it."

Vuong nodded. "Roger that, Sarge. Ooh rah."

"I think we should be going," Talmadge said, shifting nervously behind Vuong.

Baker stared at the men for a second longer before moving away from the corpses and continuing towards the end of the bay. He couldn't shake the feeling that his men were too anxious to leave. He understood, their entire unit had been killed, and they were afraid of dying themselves, but how could they risk transporting an unknown entity back with them. Unless the others had been compromised and wanted to act as transport for the alien creature… That, he couldn't allow that to happen. If it got back, then he, his family, and the rest of the world would share the same fate as the colony, and he would not, under any circumstances, allow that to happen. He had to make sure they weren't compromised, but at the moment, he struggled against the feeling that they were both beginning to act a little strange, and that had him worried. He had hoped it would have been Talmadge.

Everything was becoming so confusing.

At the back section stood a large loader and a massive pile of rock and sediment filled crates atop a row of pallets. The loader stood silently, a bright blue suit of steel and titanium, covered in a thin layer of orange dust, surrounded by dozens of steel crates. For a split second, Vuong thought of a vintage movie he had seen years back with a woman strapped into one of the machines, fighting a giant alien; the same that had been the cause of Sarge getting his nickname. He quickly realized that

that'd be useless against a monster no one could see, that killed you with your mind, not snapping teeth and a whipping tail. He realized he had been holding his breath while fantasizing about the mech versus monster fight and exhaled silently, continuing towards the massive door a few meters away. For an instant he felt embarrassed that he had entertained such childish thoughts while surrounded by the reality they were in. He shrugged it off, pushing the emotion back and continued on. "The corridor behind this door is a straight shot to the cargo bay. If all goes well, there shouldn't be anything standing in our way." He looked at Talmadge and nodded. "I'll seal this behind us. Don't want anything following us out."

Talmadge nodded, watching as the soldier made his way to the door and engaged the switch that moved the foot thick piece of steel to the side.

"Make it quick," Baker said as they passed through, slightly irritated that the company rep was giving orders, and that his men were listening to them. He was their commander, or had they suddenly forgotten that?

*"That man is the monster. The others are with him. They're helping it escape, Daddy."*

Baker flinched, his daughter's words softly warming his ear canal. He glanced to the men to see if any of them had heard her, but knew whatever creature it was that was with them, wouldn't allow them to. It didn't want them to know the truth. It needed them to help it escape. He swallowed hard. He was going home, and his family was coming with him. He chuckled silently. He was gonna have a hell of a time explaining to his men how it was that his wife and daughter had shown up on Mars, a year after they had been reported dead. He knew it was going to be a difficult conversation, but one that he would have to have. Once he told his men, they wouldn't have to hide any longer. He paused, glancing up at Talmadge who was staring at Vuong as he sealed the door. Nothing was going to stand in his way, nothing. He stared blankly, a voice in the back of his mind screaming at the top of its lungs that he was confused, that something wasn't right, that he needed to get his thoughts straight. He knew the facility was getting stronger, somehow understood that whatever creature it was that was in there with them was getting stronger with every death. But the more he struggled, the more he drifted away, an animal caught in quicksand that sunk itself deeper with every attempt to escape. He knew he had to kill the creature; could sense that there was something driving him to stay, not to get on that ship, but the moment he tried to focus on what that was, he would see his daughter's face, and feel the warmth of his wife's breath on his neck. No. He had to get free. He had to get back home. He pushed the feeling back and clenched his fists, gritting his teeth together as he continued.

The lights overhead began to flicker, a strobing pulse cascading around them as they made their way down the massive corridor. Metal creaked all around them, the station screaming in anger at their escape as they made their way quickly down the hall. Bullet holes etched the walls and spent casings skipped off their feet as they approached the section that led to hydroponics, and the cargo bay thirty yards away. Baker could feel his head pounding, the pulsing stabbing into his brain just behind his eyeballs. The migraines were getting worse, and the whispering had grown to a drowning thrum of jumbled conversations, a steady drone of voices, endless voices warped together, squirming inside his ears. Then as they approached the giant door marked *Cargo Bay*, he saw Talmadge lapse momentarily, and for the briefest of moments, the monster revealed itself.

The men approached the door, Vuong moving quickly to the panel with Fascio and Talmadge right behind him.

"The ship's in a secure unit near the airlock on the right. The code to the door is zero four two six. All we need to do is fire it up, open the roof hatch and we're as good as home. As soon as we get back I'll file the report, and we can all go on about our lives." Talmadge held his voice to a whisper, unease quieting his tone in the large hallway.

212

"It looks like someone's hacked into the door panel," Vuong said, banging his fist against the wall next to the panel. "This might take a moment."

Baker stared at the three men huddled near the door, paranoia gnawing at his mind. He could feel them plotting, their whispers crawling beneath his skin, and he fought desperately against the urge to trust them—his own men, the last of his unit. But the station itself seemed to pulse with malice, and something else, something ancient and hungry, pressed in from the shadows. Corlin had been strong, unbreakable, and yet even he had fallen—what hope did any of them have?

Vuong's fingers flew over the security panel, sweat beading on his brow, while Fascio shifted uneasily beside him, rifle clutched tight. And then, just behind them, the figure that had been Talmadge edged closer. Baker's breath caught. He saw the nails—long, black, and splitting through the skin—stretching toward his men. The hair, once neatly styled, now hung in greasy, matted clumps, falling away in sickly patches. The creature's lips peeled back, revealing fangs that flexed and glistened in the dim light.

It crept toward Fascio, who was oblivious, his back exposed. Baker's heart hammered, a cold sweat breaking out along his spine. The thing's hunger was palpable, a living shadow ready to strike. Thank God he'd gotten the code before Talmadge had changed—before this thing had taken his place. The air seemed to thicken, the lights flickering as if the station itself recoiled from what was about to happen. Baker's finger tightened on his trigger, every instinct screaming that the real horror was only just beginning.

"Fascio!" Sarge yelled, raising his rifle at the same time. "Move back!"

Fascio and Vuong spun at the sudden sound, finding Sarge ten feet away, his rifle locked on Talmadge. There was something wild in Baker's eyes—a feverish, unhinged glint—and the muscles in his neck twitched as if something inside him was trying to claw its way out.

"I got you, you son of a bitch!" he snarled, lips twisting into a grotesque smile. The carbine barked, spitting a short, brutal burst.

"Whoa!" Fascio shouted, stumbling back as Talmadge was hurled against the door, his chest erupting in a spray of crimson. The rep slid down the frame, leaving a slick trail of blood, eyes wide and glassy in death.

"Sarge! What the hell are you doing!?" Fascio's voice cracked, but Baker didn't seem to hear. Talmadge's gaze found Vuong, pupils dilating as the last breath rattled from his lungs.

Baker's voice came low and guttural, echoing in the tense silence. "Put your weapon down, Marine. That's an order." He swung the rifle toward Fascio, the barrel unwavering, his stare hollow and predatory. "That wasn't Talmadge," he insisted, voice trembling with conviction and madness. "Can't you—"

His eyes flicked to the corpse sprawled in a widening pool of blood. For a heartbeat, confusion flickered across his face, as if reality itself was slipping. It wasn't the monster he'd seen—it was just the rep, dead and human.

"...see..?" Baker's voice faltered, lost in a storm of doubt and terror.

And then, as if summoned by his unraveling mind, the whispers returned—louder, insistent, crawling through the air and gnawing at the edges of sanity. The horror in the hall thickened, as if something unseen was watching, waiting for the next to fall.

Vuong swallowed hard, desperately wanting to look to his friend, but afraid of taking his eyes off their commander. He realized in that instant how bad things had truly become. Whatever it was, was in Sergeant Thomas. "Lower the rifle," he said after a moment, realizing that somehow, he needed to get through, to diffuse the situation. The headaches, speaking about his dead family in the present tense, Talmadge. They had to play their cards very carefully. The creature was going to try anything it could to get off the station. Fortunately for him, without his assistance, there was a possibility that the creature would never get into the hold that contained the shuttle. "It's okay, Fascio," he continued, his gaze pulling away to meet his friends. "It's just Sarge. There ain't nothing in the universe strong enough to take his grumpy ass down."

Baker felt a stir of warmth rise. "I just want to get off here like you, Son. My... I just need to get home. That's all."

Fascio felt his stomach tighten, the smell of blood rising to his nostrils causing his mouth to water with an acidic bite. He looked at Vuong who told him everything he needed to know with one glance. "Okay, Sarge. I'm just a little tense. Sorry. With everything that's happened we can't be too careful." He glanced down at the rep, a stir of emotion flickering within. Then to add to the effect he scoffed, adding, "Didn't like that son of a bitch anyways."

Sarge stared at him for a moment, and then turned his gaze to the dead rep and the pool of blood that was slowly spreading outwards.

"This door's not gonna budge," Vuong said, realizing that the trip to the other entrance could buy them the time they would need to figure their situation out, and possibly create a quick resolution to it. "There's another door past hydroponics. It's not far."

"Alright," Baker replied, pulling his gaze from Talmadge's quickly cooling corpse. "Then let's move."

Vuong nodded, rising to his feet with a quick nonverbal exchange shared between him and Fascio.

"After you," Sarge replied, waiting for the two men to make their way past before following close behind.

The creature watched with cold patience as the two men turned and made their way down the corridor, oblivious to the nightmare clinging just behind. It pressed itself tightly to the one they called Sarge, its presence a parasite woven into muscle and thought. Now, with only three left, it had to be careful—so close to freedom, so close to the promise of escape.

Hunger gnawed at its core, a ravenous anticipation rippling through its stolen flesh. The taste it had sampled upon its release was nothing compared to what it sensed awaited on the distant, teeming world these men called home. Through the haze of Baker's fractured mind, it glimpsed cities, crowds, billions of fragile minds ripe for the taking. If even a fraction of the Baker creature's memories were true, then the feast ahead would be beyond anything it had ever known.

It pulsed with anticipation, its thoughts coiling around the promise of endless hosts, endless fear. Nothing would be able to stop it—not now, not with the last barriers crumbling and the way home nearly open. All it needed was to play its part a little longer, to keep the mask in place, and soon, the horror that had devoured this lonely station would be unleashed upon an entire world.

As they passed hydroponics, Fascio caught a glimmer of white; a sheet of paper held in the hand of a man lying against the wall. The handle of a screwdriver was protruding from his head, and he could see where a pen had fallen aside. Fascio approached the man and bent down, picking up the scrap of paper.

*Don't believe anyone. They all lie. It's here with us, in the dark. It's part of everything. It feeds on our death. It consumes it. It cannot escape. It's in me.*

Fascio crumbled the paper and tossed it to the ground, turning to continue.

"What did it say?" Sarge asked from behind, glancing suspiciously at the crumbled ball below.

"Nothing. Just scrap," Fascio replied, stepping towards the hallway that branched to the left.

They continued, the empty hallways pressing in on them from all sides. Vuong could feel the sergeant's gaze boring into him with every step, and waited nervously for the sound of a pistol cocking behind him. He had to do something. His mind rattled with a nervous anticipation. Whatever it was that was loose in the station, was now inside Sarge. He didn't know how it happened, or when, but he knew that the sergeant was no longer himself, and that thought agonized him. He knew with every step he took, that there was no way he could allow the sergeant to get off the station, and that meant stopping him before they reached the cargo bay, if he didn't find a bullet lodging in the back of his skull first. The stream of thoughts stung deeply, the fact that he found himself even entertaining them a harsh reminder of the situation they had been dropped into. All he wanted to do was survive and get back home. "Sarge?" he asked.

"Yeah?"

"I bet you're pretty happy to get home to your family, huh? After all this time?"

Fascio glanced at Vuong. They both knew that Sarge's family was dead. He tensed, knowing that Vuong was potentially stoking a fire that could very quickly get them both burned, baiting a creature they knew nothing about.

Baker could see his daughter's face smiling in front of him, the smell of Friday night pasta in the kitchen wafting up to his nose. His wife cooked it every week. He missed that smell. "Yeah," he replied blankly. "I miss them." He knew he had to play it off. If his men realized his family was already with him, they would try and keep them from leaving. They wouldn't understand. They were back.

Somehow, they had come back.

They reached the door.

"Sarge," Fascio said, turning around with his hand nestled against the stock of the shotgun. "You know your family's dead right? They died a year ago. You were devastated."

Baker stared at him blankly, rummaging through the cloud of thoughts that swirled in his mind; a jumble of memory flashes and overlapping voices. It was impossible. He had heard them speaking to him since he had arrived. He had seen them. They couldn't be dead, yet, somewhere, deep in his mind, he felt a pain struggling to resurface, a deep loss and anguish that told him the other was right. No... They were trying to trick him. If they could confuse him enough, he would show weakness, and if that happened, then they would turn on him. They were going to take the ship for themselves. They were going to leave him... "You don't think I know what you're doing?" he spat, hands gently raising the carbine in his grasp. He could see the crooked smile slowly spreading across the other's face, twisting at the edges beneath eyes ringed dark. No one was going to stand in his way. No one was going to keep him from leaving.

"You know it's true, Sarge," Fascio continued, watching the sergeant continue to raise the rifle. "It's this station. It gets to you. Whatever's in here with us is making you, making us, think things that aren't true. It makes you see things. I'm seeing them too, Sarge. I know it feels real, but it's not. It's this, goddamn, whatever it is. Whatever it is they let loose out there. We have to get out of here, Sarge."

Baker's vision tunneled, the world collapsing to a single, mocking face. Fascio saw the sergeant's eyes shrink to predatory slits, a jagged, unnatural grin splitting his lips—teeth bared, animal and wrong. "You can't hide now. I can see you," Baker hissed, his voice warped and barely human, arms trembling with a violence that threatened to break free. The rifle in his hands twitched, desperate for release.

A chill stabbed through Fascio's core. For a heartbeat, the sergeant's face twisted, flesh rippling with something ancient and hungry beneath the skin. Then, in a blur, Baker's carbine snapped up, the muzzle locking on Fascio's skull.

Instinct screamed. Fascio dove, the world erupting in thunder and muzzle flash. Bullets shredded the air where his head had been, splinters of metal and wall biting his cheek. He crashed to the ground, rolling, shotgun already in his grip. In a single, desperate motion, he swung up and fired.

The blast was deafening. Baker's head vanished in a spray of bone and blood, painting the wall in a grotesque mural. The sergeant's body crumpled, twitching, then lay still—a ruined heap, neck spurting blood in sick, rhythmic pulses. The stench of burnt powder and iron filled the corridor, thick and suffocating.

Fascio staggered upright, ears ringing, heart pounding so hard it hurt. He stared at the corpse—the man who had led him through hell, now reduced to a twitching, blood-soaked shell. Numb with shock, he watched as the air above the body seemed to recoil, a thin, oily vapor writhing and twisting in the flickering light, as if the horror itself refused to die.

"There!" Vuong's scream shattered the paralysis. He raised his rifle, firing wildly at the shimmering distortion that slithered upward, bullets sparking off metal and vanishing into the gloom.

Fascio spun, racking his shotgun and firing at the thing—at the impossible, shifting shape that seemed to scream without sound. The air vibrated with a silent, psychic shriek, a pressure that stabbed into their skulls and set their teeth on edge. The shape flickered, then shot down the corridor, vanishing into the shadows at the edge of the light.

For a moment, only the echo of gunfire and the coppery tang of blood remained. Vuong stood frozen, eyes wide and unblinking, sweat beading on his brow. "You think I got it?" he whispered, voice trembling, but the darkness offered no answer—only the certainty that something still watched, and waited, just beyond the reach of their lights.

Fascio stared into the empty hallway, his breath still held in his lungs for a moment before expelling it in a gust. "I don't know. Let's just get the hell out of here."

Vuong slapped the door latch and there was a loud groan as the large hatch slid to the side. Metal scraped metal, and for a moment the inside of the bay was pitch black. Then with a flicker, the overhead lights came to life and a bright illumination filled the room. They made their way in and Vuong turned to hit the panel to close the door behind him. As he did he saw the fragmented plastic and metal where someone had broken the seal from the other side in an effort to keep someone or something from getting in. "Shit," he whispered, glancing back down the hall.

"Doesn't matter. Let's just get the fuck out of here." He paused, scanning the cargo bay. "Now where the hell's that ship?"

Vuong turned around, pointing to a cargo hold near the back of the bay. "Should be that one."

Fascio turned and started quickly for the door, slapping Vuong on the arm as he passed. "Come on!"

They made their way quickly through the empty bay, moving as quickly as they could. They could feel the station tensing all around them, hissing and angry, screaming through groans of metal and snapping cables. Vuong punched in the code and the door slowly opened, the seconds taking years while they waited. Sitting inside the large hold was a transport ship, slightly smaller than the one they had arrived on, but much newer. Vuong glanced behind him, staring into the space between them and the door. Then he turned and made his way quickly to the shuttle. He pulled a cable from his holowrist and connected it with a port on the shuttle's landing gear. Instantly the ship's controls popped up in front of him. He primed the engine and lowered the outer hatch. The moment steel touched steel he was up the ramp and turning to seal the door behind them.

*Don't believe anyone. They all lie. It's here with us, in the dark. It's part of everything. It feeds on our death. It consumes it. It cannot escape. It's in me.*

"Whatever it was that killed the colonists, it was inside of Sarge," Fascio said, stopping at the top of the ramp. "The note I found, it said not to believe anyone, that everyone was infected. I don't know what it meant, but it said that it fed on their death, that it consumed it. What if we're infected too?"

Vuong stared at him from inside the ship. He couldn't shake the feeling as well, the cold pressure of something foreign sitting just inside his mind. But they had managed to make it the entire way to the ship, had survived, and he wasn't going to give up now. "Look, man. When we get home, we can tell them everything that happened. We'll let them know, we'll go through quarantine procedure or whatever else they need to give us a clean bill. But I'm not staying here. Fuck that. We can deal with it then."

"I just don't want anyone else to die..."

"Me neither, Fas," Vuong replied as gently as he could, his gaze flashing to the empty space behind him. "But we will if you don't get your ass in here and seal that hatch. Or at least one of us will, and the other will end up bringing that thing back with them, and we can't allow that to happen. So come on, man, let's get the hell out of here!" Fascio stood on the ramp, staring at the floor for a moment as a frigid chill moved through him. "I thought Sarge was stronger than that."

Vuong engaged the hatch, raising the ramp and sealing the door as Fascio moved next to him. Then he moved as quickly as he could to the pilot's station and buckled in, engaging the roof hatch and bringing the instrument panel to life. The console illuminated before him and the vid screen flashed to life, the walls of the hold filling the monitor.

"I really thought I was gonna die here," Fascio said, taking a seat next to him. "I thought... I thought I was never going to escape this planet."

"Me neither," Vuong said, finishing the last of the ignition sequence before engaging the thrusters and lifting the shuttle into the air. "How about we go home."

21

The planet sat resting below, a vast ball of orange and red; motionless as the shuttle drifted in orbit. From where they sat it looked peaceful, almost calm. There was no station, no death, just an endless sea of burnt crimson spreading from one end of the horizon to the other. The air in the cabin hung heavy, a thick cloud of sadness saturated with loss. Vuong and Fascio had fallen silent the moment they lifted off, the feeling of relief refusing to surface behind the last two days of panic laced fear. The memories of their comrades wore heavy on them and both sat lost in an inconsolable haze. Vuong had sent a series of distress calls out and logged a detailed report of the events that had unfolded at the station. The words, void of emotion and detail had left him drained, eyes red and puffed from pent up tears finally released. He had slipped away to a private section to allow his grief to be expelled. When he had finished, he made his way back to the bridge and finished plotting their course back to Earth. He engaged the autopilot and leaned back in his chair as the ship corrected course and the thrusters ignited, pulling them further out of orbit and onto a course that would have them back on Earth a short cryosleep away. He stared at the vid-screen, watching the planet slowly shrink to a dot in the distance, then he took a deep breath and shut the view screen off, turning to look at Fascio, who stared back.

"They're gonna think we're crazy," Fascio said after a moment.

"Well, it doesn't help that the only proof we had was inside Talmadge's pocket." Vuong replied, taking a deep breath and exhaling slowly at the thought of the hearings they would have to sit through upon returning, and the inquisition the board was going to host.

Vuong felt a thin chill work through him. His friend was right. They had no quarantine protocol, no tests, no way to know if either of them was infected, and with all that had happened, it was easily quite so. They had no choice but to escape and hope that whatever threat it was that had slowly picked them off, had been killed in that hallway, or at least left trapped in the station.

Vuong stared at him from across the seat. "Have you heard the whispers?"

Fascio nodded. "Yeah."

"Have you seen anything that could only have been a hallucination; no matter how much your mind tried to rationalize it?"

The little boy standing in the room flashed in his memory, but as he struggled with the picture, wasn't sure if he'd actually seen it, or simply imagined it. "Yeah..."

"And are you now?"

"No. Not since when we left."

227

"Me neither. So, since the whispering has stopped, and neither of us is trying to kill each other, I'd say it's pretty safe to assume that we aren't... infected... or, possessed." He paused. "Think about it. Sarge started talking about his family as if they were still alive. He was already acting strange. You're acting pretty normal, and I'd like to think I am too. I know I'm not seeing dead relatives, or hearing any voices telling me to kill you, or myself. I think whatever it was that was responsible, we shot it full of holes and it's dead in that hallway, or at the least, still trapped in there. Or maybe we just had to kill whoever it was in for it to die? All I know, is we made it out of there, and we're still alive."

"Tch," Fascio scoffed, turning his head to the blank space where the view screen had been moments before. "Somehow I don't think it was that easy. I mean, whatever that thing was, had been inside that pyramid for how long? Thousands of years...? No. It's still there. They need to nuke that station from orbit and pray that even that works." A thin ripple worked up his arms at the thought. "It wasn't just some virus, man. That thing thought, it hunted. Whatever the hell it was, had survived for who knows how long. Something like that doesn't survive by being stupid. That thing knew exactly what it was doing." He paused, shaking his head twice. "No. They're gonna send another crew there, probably another unit. I just hope to god they receive our communications before they do, and that they actually listen." Again, he paused, his gaze falling to the vid-screen. "Something tells me I'm hoping for too much though…"

"There's no way the company's gonna blow up a trillion dollar investment like that; based off the words of a couple low paid grunts. No. They're gonna send another unit back down there, I just hope we managed to take care of whatever that thing was. Hopefully, it's just a cleanup job."

Vuong stood up, stretching his hands towards the ceiling. "No matter. I'm glad I won't be there when they do."

"Yeah," Fascio said, rising to his feet. "Me too."

Vuong turned and made his way to the cryo-sleep chamber. He made his way down the hall, sterile light brushing past him as he entered the sterile room. Slowly he undressed, prepping himself for the dreamless journey, thankful for the first time that his sleep would be nothing but an unconscious black, and when he woke up, the station, the death, would be millions of miles away. He took his clothes off and climbed into the pod. Slowly he situated himself, his gaze falling from one empty pod to another against the wall. Again, a deep pain pierced through him. Portofino, Corlin, Wilkes, DiLeonardo, Thomas… Each name played syllable by syllable in his mind, the accompanying voices playing softly behind. He watched as Fascio undressed, assuming the same emotions were wracking him as well. The room felt cold and lonely around them, and the sense of relief at surviving still refused to set in.

Around them, the ship vibrated softly, the low thrum of the hyperdrive thrusters hovering almost unnoticeably in the background. Vuong could feel the persistent headache beginning to fade and looked forward to it being gone when they resurrected. Stress, fatigue, panic. He knew it was going to be a while until his body managed to regulate itself again. "I'll see you in the morning," he said as he reached out to engage the switch that would lower the capsule's lid. "And yeah, I think it's time we put in for transfer."

"Roger that," Fascio replied. "Roger, that."

The lid to the capsule closed, latching shut with a soft click, a thin vapor filling the interior as the atmosphere was vented and replaced with one that slowed the body's functions, turning seconds into sleepless weeks and dreamless, frozen months.

Across the room, Fascio looked at his friend and took a deep breath, exhaling heavily as he closed and latched the pod's lid. He felt a shiver run through him as the lid locked into place. As the air vented a thin hiss whispered past his ear, a vapor of stale breath mixing with the slightly bitter atmosphere that filled the pod. Sleep tugged at him, pressing heavy against his eyes. He felt his breaths slowing, the gentle prickling of release as his body began its chemically induced relaxation. As he began to drift further away, the edges of his sight fading to a foggy white, his gaze moved to his friend, already fast asleep across the room. He blinked slowly, his vision fading in and out, when in a single moment of focus, he saw a faint distortion next to his friend, a small ripple that shifted inside the translucent pod.

The shuttle continued on course, a silent craft, drifting through the endless void. Inside, the lights had gone dark, the only systems still active the ones needed to maintain direction and sustain life still active. The room the cryopods were in was quiet, a thin layer of beeping in the air as the systems that regulated hypersleep and vitals ran automatically. Beneath that, a series of dull thuds, almost inaudible, repeated frantically; fists pounding against the inside of the hyper-sleep chamber lid. Then the pounding slowed and came to a stop as cryosleep took over and the captive marine was pulled into the dreamless black.

TRANSMISSION: OUT

www.ingramcontent.com/pod-product-compliance
Lightning Source LLC
Chambersburg PA
CBHW031952240626
47153CB00003B/958